Escaping Avila Chase

M.K. Williams

Printed in the United States of America
First Printing, 2016 The Games You Cannot Win
Publisher: MK Williams Publishing, LLC

Library of Congress Control Number: 2021915167
ISBN :
978-1-7333929-8-3 (eBook)
978-1-952084-12-6 (Paperback)

Mary K. Williams
https://1mkwilliams.com
1mkwilliams author@gmail.com

All Persons Fictitious Disclaimer:
This book is a work of fiction. Any similarity between the characters and situations within its pages and places or persons, living or dead, is unintentional and co-incidental. Any names used that happen to match the name of a real person is either coincidental or intended as a compliment.

Works by M.K. Williams

Fiction

The Project Collusion Series
Nailbiters
Architects

The Feminina Series
The Infinite-Infinite
The Alpha-Nina

Other Fiction
The Games You Cannot Win
Interview with a #Vanlifer
Enemies of Peace

Non-Fiction

Self-Publishing for the First-Time Author
Book Marketing for the First-Time Author
How to Write Your First Novel: A Guide for Aspiring Fiction Authors
Going Wide: Self-Publishing Your Books Outside The Amazon Ecosystem
Author Your Ambition: The Complete Self-Publishing Workbook for First-Time Authors

M.K. Williams

DEDICATION

To Thomas F. Bissonette

CONTENTS

1 Escaping Avila Chase 1

2 Author's Note 85

3 Acknowledgments 88

Escaping Avila Chase

It was cold.

Or rather, it was cool. The morning air was just a shade below a comfortable temperature as I sauntered home along South Street. It was the afterglow of summer in Philadelphia where fall was just starting to loom in the early morning hours. The day would still be warm enough, but that morning was too cool for the t-shirt and jeans that I was wearing. The same that I had been wearing since the night before. Or, had only temporarily removed. Nonetheless, I was underdressed, a little exposed, and walking at a fast clip to make it back to my apartment so I could shower, shave, and get to the office on time.

I didn't often make a habit of going out to bars on work-nights, but the previous night had been a Sunday and I was stuck with the option of staying in and contemplating my current misery or going out to drown my sorrows in whiskey. I had chosen the latter. And as fortune would favor me, the evening had turned out to my benefit as a friendly woman of loose morals took me home for the evening. I was able to forget my troubles in her embrace. However, by morning, all of my worries had caught up to me, as though they were watching me through the unfamiliar apartment windows, begging for me to try and shut them out.

With each clop of my shoes on the concrete sidewalk, I retraced my thoughts and intentions, not only of the previous night, but of the previous decade. I was a man haunted and I could still feel that ghost hovering just behind me, beckoning me to turn around and confront my sins.

I passed the small bakeries with delicious aromas steaming through the open doors, sandwich shops that wouldn't open until the afternoon, and tourist kiosks that became more prominent as I worked my way towards the Broad Street line.

My feet carried me quickly down the tiled stairs, through the turnstile, and onto the car heading north within seconds. My luck must have been keeping up with me. As the car trundled down the tracks, I took one of the empty seats and found myself staring at a gray and brown reflection of myself, only some of my features illuminated against the passing concrete walls of the subway system. My immediate thought was to notice how exhausted I looked. I was quick to remind myself that I was wearing the exhaustion of a man who had just gotten laid, so I tried to shrug off my continued feeling of self-loathing. That particular feeling would only creep up and crawl onto my skin whenever I thought about *her*. And that is exactly what I had been doing that morning. And the night before that. And the night before that.

It wasn't the girl who had taken me home that was on my mind. She was nice enough and pretty enough, but not anyone that I wanted to see again. Lenore, that was the name of the woman who had taken pity on me at the bar. She was kind and one-of-a-million bottle blondes with

Tastykake padded thighs and an atrocious accent. She had given me her number earlier in the evening, but after a few more drinks she was desperately hinting as her willingness to take me home. I inspected the scrap of paper with her phone number on it quickly as I dressed that morning. Her twos were sloppy, excessively curvy and likely a little too indistinguishable. Her one begged for further clarification. It wasn't any "l" or "I" or numeral of some kind, but instead it was a resolute hash-mark. It looked like one of many days of a prison sentence. And her five must have usually been clear and distinct, but on this scrap of paper it only looked like an "s." I looked at the crumpled corner of a napkin that had been hastily ripped and written on, and re-crumpled it gently. With delicate precision I placed it directly below where my jeans had hung across Lenore's kitchen chair, so that it would look as though it had accidentally fallen out. It would be an innocent enough reason for me to have 'lost' her number and completely remove my need to call or feel remorseful for not reaching out to her again.

I recall now that I had been smiling at this thought, pleased at my own little trick, when I looked up, through the subway window, and directly into the eyes of the one woman I was trying to forget the most. No surprise, there she was. Watching me, looking out at me as though I was on a wanted poster and she was studying my features so that she could report me at any second. But she was the one on the poster. Those damned posters that had been up for two weeks now and had brought on my most recent bought of drinking and guilt-ridden sleepless nights.

Those piercing green eyes were at bus stops, in the windows at local shops, and generally all over the city. I could see her eyes judging me, as though she had summoned some hateful memory of me when the photo had been taken. Most other people would just recognize the eyes as female, clear green, and unyielding. They may even recognize their owner, most locals would. I'm talking, of course, about our latest Philadelphian sensation. A home-town girl who made it big. The same one who left my heart under her boot heel in the process.

You would think that after almost a decade I'd be over it. She was the hardest one to get rid of and naturally, the one I just couldn't shake. That morning I should have been able to shake her from my mind, focus on the beginning of another busy work-week, and just plug-on without giving her another thought. But she was there. Haunting me as ever. Finally, the car pulled away and I stood, waiting for the next stop to rush out before the morning commuters really began to pile in.

Once I got off the subway, through the maze of hallways and stairs at 15th and Market, I made my way up through Dilworth Plaza and cut across to Walnut quickly. I walked up to 18th and turned quickly to enter my building. The chill of the morning was still stuck to my skin and I wanted to get inside before I started to get a runny nose.

In the shower I tried not to let my mind wander again. I couldn't afford a luxurious soul-searching shower; I needed a quick rinse-down before heading to the office. I decided I could handle a little scruff and some smart-guy comments about the thin layer of gristle on my chin. Once I had changed into my suit, combed through my hair, and grabbed an apple, I felt the routine of Monday morning starting to settle in. I put on my black leather shoes, tied the laces quickly, and began to eat my apple as I strolled back down to the ground level and out into the morning. The sun was starting to warm the concrete. Something about that moment felt very peaceful to me. Maybe I was relieved to be wearing longer layers to keep myself warm since I hate to be cold. Maybe it was the natural sugar from the apple that was beginning to perk up my system. Maybe it was the after-effects of a pleasurable evening. I still haven't pinpointed what made me feel so good. But I do recall that

I did feel very good, and that it was such a stark contrast to how I had felt before, and also after, that moment.

Because just as I was working my way through the familiar streets of my city, I was confronted, once again, with not only a poster, but a huge banner highlighting my worst fear.

Perhaps I should start to enlighten you as to my plight. I had been on the wrong end of a bad break-up many years earlier. Even though I had experienced some other failed relationships since then, likely stemming from my inability to get over this root-event, this particular romance had left a scar beyond measure. And the havoc it was wreaking continued to spill across new layers of my life. The messiest of all romantic ends was with Miss Avila Chase. Yes, the one with the Scarlet Moore paranormal mystery series. *Oh, you've read them? You think they're just fantastic? Screw you.*

She may smile pretty for her interviews and press releases now, but I've seen the scowl that she hides. That hideous mug she makes when she cries. Followed by her face that gets pink with anger as her eyes turn from sea to crystalline green. She was so stubborn. She just had to win, she always had to be right. So, I left her and just as I expected then, this icky, scratching, uncomfortable guilt has been with me for years. That feeling was subtle at first, but in the months leading up to that specific morning as I chewed my apple and hurried to work, it had blossomed into an unwieldy mass that I could not bear. My arms were spread out like Atlas trying to carry that heavy guilt, my legs quivering from the strain of it. Even with the early morning sun and my fresh breakfast, I could not escape the panic imposed by her memory.

What might cause this anxiety you ask? Well, her latest novel, #10 in the series, was due to hit bookshelves at the end of that week. The series was an international hit and because she was from Philadelphia, *my city*, the city that she left when we were over, she was getting significant local attention. She was kicking off her book-tour with a large party and book signing that upcoming Friday. At the bookstore just down the block. The banner proclaiming the midnight release party was going up just as I was beginning to savor that brief and happy moment. I shook my head and pressed on.

At first, her books had gone unnoticed. Avila had signed on to a disadvantageous deal with a literary agent the year before we met. She cranked out her first masterpiece only to have it edited within an inch of its life and panned by all of the critics. She became convinced that if her work had not been shredded by the publishing house that it would have performed better. She found a way out of her contract and began to work on the second and third books in the series.

Enter me, Trevor Hobbertson. When we first met and Avila explained that she was a writer of novels, I half expected her to confess that she wrote penny-store romance novels or erotic re-writes of popular fiction. I was relieved to know that her focus was on mysteries and the para-normal or super-normal, or hypo-normal.

Our relationship must have been fated to fail because when we met, she was already involved with two others: *Scarlett Moore and the Invasion of the Hidden Tomb* and *Scarlett Moore and the Nirvana Paradox*. Those books were her lovers, her something on the side of our relationship. At first, like in most relationships, it was pleasant and happy. I was so proud of her work and relished each opportunity she gave for me to proofread her latest chapters, scan for any continuity issues. I was her go-to guy.

Each book followed the adventures and mishaps of a museum curator turned paranormal activity detective: Scarlett Moore. Think female Indiana Jones meets X-Files. Avila was always such a history nerd; she poured so many nuanced details into each book. I would never admit this to anyone who asks me directly, but I think the stories are actually great. However, my official public position is that: "I don't much care for her little stories, same as I don't care for the doodles of strangers on coffee napkins."

But I digress.

Each novel in the series revealed a new paranormal mystery. Intertwined into the subplot was Scarlett's love life, which always left something to be desired. There was also frequent reference to Scarlett's overly affectionate cat: Nibbles. Avila always tried to vary how much she played up these secondary lines. The first novel, *Scarlett Moore and the Wondrous Mystery of the Nile*, which I read after our second date so that I could ask her more about it, was perfunctory. I could see why Avila was so indignant with the publishing house. When we moved in together after 3 months of dating, she came with her clothes, shoes, pots, pans, and two boxes full of unsold copies of her debut novel.

It was easy then to be crushed for her. I took a box to work and pressured my coworkers into buying the book. I was like one of those obnoxious dads pushing Girl Scout cookies on their colleagues, only I was peddling for my girlfriend. To this day, I don't know if any of them read that book, and I don't care. I was a doting and attentive boyfriend. I understand that the description is entirely self-serving at this point, but it was true.

As the second and third books progressed, I helped her out as best as I could. However, a startling trend began to emerge in the secondary plot lines. In the first novel, Scarlett Moore was thrown into her first adventure when an overseas vacation with her then-boyfriend went a little haywire. Flash forward to the ending, the boyfriend was an international art smuggler. *Tisk tisk. Bad boyfriend.*

This began my torture and reverie. While enjoying a leisurely glass of wine one evening, Avila was telling me about her only trip abroad when she was still in college. She was flowing through some anecdote about how she lost a hat in St. Mark's Square in Venice when she abruptly ended her story. I was curious as to the sudden change.

"Well, then what happened?" I had asked so innocently, taking in my last swallow of Burgundy.

"Nothing, I bought a new hat. I think I actually lost it on another trip so maybe I should keep this up as a running in-joke." Avila brushed off her story quickly and I could see in her eyes that she didn't want me to ask any more questions. But of course, I did.

"So, were you there alone?" I finally hit a nerve because her eyes darted around the room, searching for anything to fix on rather than look me in the eyes. She sipped on the wine in front of her, trying to look casual, but helplessly caught in my snare.

"No, I was with a friend," another sip of wine, a quick motion to get off the couch and refill my glass.

"Which friend?" I was being playful, I was being coy, I was being the irresistible self that had made her like butter in my hands so many times.

"Oh, you don't know 'em," she waved her hand as if she was swatting the question away like a mosquito. Her words were slightly hard to understand as she rushed through her answer and headed into the kitchen. But I heard the one word she had tried to conceal the most.

"A 'him' is it?" I was in a playful mood; I wanted to see how uncomfortable this might make her feel. I pressed on.

"Yep," she said quickly. Her eyes were so focused on not meeting mine, it was so cute and funny, but a little worrisome. The more that she kept trying to push off her answer the more worried I became. "My ex, Anthony."

She had never mentioned her exes before, but neither had I. We hadn't gotten to the point of openly discussing our past relationships: what went wrong, what pet peeves we had inherited from them, what we blamed ourselves for in each messy end. Hearing his name for the first time was a little rattling.

I relented after I saw how uncomfortable she became. We finished our wine and discussed other topics. The thought kept picking at my synapses; begging for me to look deeper and find out why she had been so coy, so sealed about it that she had stopped mid-thought rather than let his name slip. Why had it taken so much prodding to find out this small detail?

Being the regular snoop that I am, I took a little time to search for this Anthony. I guess I could say 'well it is my job,' but none of my duties for the F.B.I. require or remotely imply that Facebook stalking my girlfriend's ex-boyfriend is part of the job. Surely, my many exes would have liked to be able to check up on my trail of failed attempts at monogamy before I met them. *Oh well.*

A quick search quickly revealed an 'Anthony Smith.' He was handsome and tan, but I wasn't feeling insecure because of his appearance. No, it was a thin line of text that began to play through my mind, as though Avila was reciting directly from her book:

> *It was the summer adventure of a lifetime with Aaron. Scarlett could hardly contain her giddy excitement at the idea of a European vacation with her college sweetheart. Would he propose? Would he drop to one knee, his thick black hair catching in the wind, his dark as night brown eyes twinkling with love? Scarlett could only imagine what her tanned and handsome boyfriend-perhaps fiancé- would look like as they savored each moment of their trip, and each evening with each other.*
>
> *-Scarlett Moore and the Wondrous Mystery of the Nile*

I couldn't help but compare the written description of the supposedly fictional Aaron and the real-life Anthony Smith. Perhaps it was all a coincidence. Many men have dark hair, and dark eyes, and could tan in the summer. Pssh- nothing to worry about, I kept telling myself.

But, with each chapter that I helped to review for her subsequent novels, I could tell that the love interests for Scarlett were following an odd trend: they were horrible to her, they were untrustworthy, they were devastatingly handsome, and they all met a bad end either by law enforcement or an unsavory death by their own ignorance or negligence.

The last piece of the puzzle fell into place a month or so later. An off-hand comment from one of Avila's close friends at some party sealed our fate. The truth that was revealed those many years ago had brought me to that present moment of despair and pained annoyance as I hurried to work, wiping away the juice that flowed from the apple onto my chin.

The comment that was made at the party had been innocent enough. This friend, whose name I can't even remember, was going on about how she was so happy that Avila had found me. This friend was so happy because Avila's most recent ex, Roman, had left her in a negative tailspin of a break-up. Sure enough, a quick search revealed a man by the same name. His picture matched the description of the Reginald Thompson that had been featured in the second and third installments of the Scarlett Moore novels.

I could have let it go. I should have let it go. But I had to know more. As more time passed, Avila and I had grown closer, our relationship more solid and established. I simply couldn't leave it alone. I wanted to understand what compelled her to do as I suspected, to write her ex-boyfriends into her novels. *Why couldn't she let it be? Was she unable of creating villains out of thin air? Did she use her reality as a crutch with which to craft her fiction? Would I become a story at a later date?*

One evening, after a homemade dinner, we stood in our small apartment kitchen. Me, cleaning the dishes, and Avila standing to my left waiting for wet dishes to dry. Our familiar routines were the comfortable knitting that started to warm my cold heart, but the fabric soon began to itch and irritate me. This was the first of many "itchings."

The conversation began innocently enough. "I think I am ready to start writing out my ideas for the next novel." She had only recently finished the manuscripts to the second and third Scarlett Moore stories and mentioned that she needed a break from Scarlett for a bit.

"Oh yeah, where will Miss Moore be going this time?" I asked, genuinely curious as to what she would come up with. I was impressed by her creativity, something I will no longer admit to.

"I'm still taking a break from Scarlett. I think I want to write a murder-mystery." I could tell by her voice, the way she put a nervous emphasis on the second clause, that she was looking for some validation of her new endeavor. I couldn't deny that my own literary tastes were a bit more masculine: suspense, thriller, mystery. Technically women write in these genres as well, but I tend to find that I only prefer to read male authors.

"I'd like to read that," I was genuine and smiled at this. But my next thought slipped out too quickly. "Although, I'd like to find out what happens with Scarlett and Roman." *Whoops*. I had been translating the text of her books in my mind, everywhere I saw the name 'Reginald', I was automatically thinking 'Roman,' and picturing the face I had seen online. This was the first time that I had vocalized this thought and it was a mistake.

"What?" she reacted quickly.

"I mean Scarlett and Reginald," I was transparent, it was a foolish lie to tell. It must have been that soft fabric of our relationship beginning to nag and chaff.

"No, you said Roman." By now, she had placed the dish that was in her hands on the counter with extreme care, holding her composure as clearly as she could.

I hesitated to release the thoughts that I had been

bottling up. Then, I let it out. "I know that you have been using your exes as characters in your books. I know how things ended with Anthony or should I say, Aaron."

"Oh, you know how things ended?" Her arms crossed and her eyebrows furrowed quickly. She was in her animalistic attack position.

"I know that you're still hung up on your ex-boyfriend, why else would you be writing him into your books?" I broke out into my Philadelphian ways, gesturing with my hands to emphasize my point, as though the cabinet that my hand was directed at somehow contained evidence to prove my point.

"That's not it at all, Trevor." She was calculated in her answer. She had more that she wanted to say, but she didn't let it slip.

"Oh really? Then why are you spending all this time having Scarlett go around and have these romances with Roman?!" I laid out the evil and green venom that was in me.

"What? I'm not Scarlett, Trevor. And Reginald isn't Roman. If you're jealous about some guy that I'm not with anymore, that's on you. If you want to talk through this, we can. But I'm not going to stand here and have you yell your paranoid theories at me." She started to walk away. I knew that I had lost because as much as I tried to play it cool, I was jealous.

"Okay, so what if I am jealous?" She had already moved into the living room, sitting on the patterned and faded sofa, facing away from me. I stood in the doorway between the kitchen and the living room. Not really in the same space as her, but not specifically in the other space. This would be the limbo I would learn to live in.

"Why? Things didn't end well with Roman; it's not like I'm hoping we'd get back together. And I'm with you!" I could see that she was shaken by what I was saying.

"Then why is your character described to look exactly

like him?" I knew she couldn't deny that.

She let out an exasperated sigh. I could see I had caught her in a thought, but then it must have shaken free from her because she turned her face quickly. "Wait, do you know Roman?"

"No, but I can do a Facebook search, Avila." I was moving closer to her; I didn't like the forced space between us.

"You've been stalking my ex-boyfriend on Facebook?" She was only getting more frustrated. I was stubborn and had to prove my point.

"Oh, like you haven't gone through my old photos and tried to see what my ex looked like?" She didn't respond to that one.

"Why-," she changed sentences while speaking, "where is this all coming from?" She was rubbing the spot right between her eyebrows; was she really getting a headache from this conversation? That motion was her tell, or maybe she was just playing me. I wouldn't put it past her, now that I have hindsight to better inform my memory. She could have been feigning a headache just so that I would drop the subject.

"I can read Avila. If you're writing your ex into your novel, then you clearly aren't over him." I tried to emphasize my point once again with my hands. It didn't seem to help my argument in the end.

"But I am. If I wasn't, I wouldn't be able to still talk to him." She said it as though these words were supposed to soothe me somehow.

It took me a moment to compose my next thought. "Wait, you still talk to Roman? Like on a regular basis?"

"Yes, we're friends." Avila looked at me like I had just asked her what year it was or who the president was, as though I was an uninformed time traveler hoping to catch-up with a temporal loop.

"How close of friends? You haven't mentioned hanging

out with him once since we've been together?" Now I felt like an interrogator, I needed to know the details so that I could assess the situation fully.

"I talk to him a couple of times a year. We just keep in touch, that is all." She shrugged off this piece of information as thought it was so casual and banal.

"Well, why? Things are over and done between the two of you, why keep in touch?"

"That is oversimplifying things. We've shared some hard times together, he's the only other person that understands that tragedy. We can't shut each other out." Avila acted as though I had suggested not breathing oxygen for an extended period. Or as if I had implied that she could easily spend a week walking on her hands. The absurdity of my words apparent on her face.

"Why don't you try me? I can try to understand you; I can work to be that person for you." I was pleading, and this, quite clearly now, was the point of fracture.

"I don't see why you're so upset over my fictional characters and now you're upset over my friends?"

"I'm upset that you write these hot scenes between two fictional characters that seem a lot like you and your ex, Roman. And I'm frustrated that you have been all buddy-buddy with him without telling me." Honesty, while it may be advertised as refreshing, is often just a noxious as bleach. Honesty was ripping us apart. It is effective, but at what cost?

"Don't you trust me?" My recollection of the soft way that she spoke those words would galvanize my resolve in the moments that I would experience later on, as I slithered from one relationship to the next.

"I do, but- " I was about to just come right out and say it, and I did. "What is more important to you? Our relationship, or your friendship with Roman?"

She had given me the answer that I wanted at the time, but within the next four months, we were finished. Being friends with Roman was more important to her. That might not have been the final straw for her, but it was the first of many to snap and shift the weight on our backs.

So, why did any of this matter as the world prepared for her latest novel? My ex-girlfriend wrote her books about her ex-boyfriends, whether she would admit it or not. Big deal, right?

Well, as you know, she started a rapid-fire publishing schedule about ten years ago (the year after we split). This allowed her to shoot to the top of every best-seller list. I couldn't turn any corner, or scroll through a news feed without seeing her, or a reference to her books, or the upcoming movie deals. Then abruptly, two years ago, there was only silence. Not a prose piece, not a book review, not an interview, nothing. It was the most peaceful time I had ever experienced.

Until that summer, when her publicity juggernaut started up again. The latest novel by Avila Chase would be released at the end of that week. All of my educated deduction skills indicated that I would be featured in this fiction. I hadn't been adapted into a character in her other novels, surely this new novel would be the one where she decided to cast me as the villain. I had been agonizing over how she would depict me. Would she state that some mysterious and ultimately evil man had "muted blue eyes with flecks of steely grey?" or would she refer to my "uniquely metered swagger" and the "loping swing of my gait"? I might be called out by the description of my hair, "blonde and matted, flopping on the top of my head at a playful angle," or the "harsh contrast of hallowed dark bags under my eyes." Perhaps she might only make allusions to me by calling out my "jolting habit of cracking my knuckles with loud and distinct pops," or my "unfortunate and untimely allergy" to the most ridiculous of fruits.

The constant speculation was draining. I waned and

waxed like the phases of the moon between denial, acceptance, and hopeless bargaining with my unconscious mind. It made me wish that whiskey in my morning coffee wasn't frowned-upon. It was shaping up to be one hell of a Monday.

By the time I had arrived at the office, swiped my security badge, and made it through the maze of desks to my cubicle, I was going through the motions of the day and already beginning to forget the colorful start to my morning. As my standard-issue computer booted, I grabbed my trusty mug and headed to the break room for coffee where there was, as usual, a small group of other agents and admins loitering as they waited for the latest pot to finish brewing. I did the math quickly and six people waiting for coffee with a four-cup machine would put me at least another 20 minutes out from a fresh cup. I headed back to my desk and figured that if I really needed the pick-me-up, I would head back to the break room in a bit. Given my level of stress, lack of sleep, and all-around miserable demeanor that day, I really should have waited for the coffee. The dopamine drip of the caffeine into my system would have assuaged the headache that was setting in.

The headache was the result of a long-established morning routine in which I consumed a moderate amount of caffeine, my minor hangover, and the recently developed habit of grinding my teeth at night. The habit was actually a resurrected behavior. It began in those final months with Avila and persisted for the following year. Without really trying, it abated and had lied dormant until the announcement of the new book, *Scarlett: Avenged.*

While I was distracting myself from the throb of my headache and the various contributing factors, I began to thumb through the top files on my desk. I had been successful in completely forgetting about work over the weekend and needed a bit of a jog on my memory. *Ah, right, gift card fraud.*

You may scoff at the idea, but where there is the opportunity for money to change hands, there is always the opportunity for fraud. I had been working a solid stream of gift card fraud since that previous spring. As the seasons of that year evolved, I began to develop a knack for identifying and putting an end to significant operations.

When I tell people that I work for the FBI, I can see that their minds fill with pictures of secret missions, bullet proof vests, drawn hand-guns, and unnecessary danger. I was relegated, however, to the Financial Crimes division. When I began working for the Bureau, I was assisting on insurance fraud cases and other white-collar crimes. Having been able to develop a penchant for cracking electronic funds fraud, I was able to make myself a little niche. Work had been steady, and while others in law enforcement may wish for a day when people would just obey the laws and stop causing trouble, I didn't mind the job stability.

What I had been able to identify was the two main abuses for these gift cards. I'm not talking about $25 to iTunes or even $100 to Outback Steakhouse. The main cards that are used for fraud are certain kinds of the American Express or Visa gift cards. They work just like a debit card, but they have a fixed amount. *You have a relative who needs money?* Buy one of these cards and put on the amount they need; you pay a small processing fee, but you have some protection as long as you save the activation codes. Once the money is spent, the person can get rid of the card or refill it. Most people use them innocently enough.

The first main area for excessive use and re-use are the credit-card churners. They are hungry for travel rewards miles and purchase the gift cards on their shiny new plastic to meet the bonus point thresholds within the short time given. The churners use the gift cards to pay their bills, groceries, anything. Some are able to transfer the money back to their bank accounts to be able to pay for the credit card bill. In all, the churners lose the five-dollar transaction fee with each card. Technically, nothing illegal was done. But credit card companies were starting to catch on. The hay-day of churning was drawing to an end. While that method abuses the system, these churners were making the most of open loopholes and it was not illegal, so they were all good by me and Bureau.

The area that I focused on was the small-time thieves that were preying on dear granny, or anyone naïve enough to hand over cash for a gift card, without asking too many questions. Did you ever hear a story like this 20 or so years ago? A friend, an acquaintance, or just a person on the street says that they need cash. They have lost all of their credit cards and as odds would have it only have their checkbook on them. Because not all stores will accept a check, they are in a bind, but they swear that they are good for the money. The gullible party hands over their cash in exchange for a check that would bounce.

Well, with these gift cards the party that is "in-a-bind" is handing over a gift card in exchange for cash and making off with the money. Because these cards can hold up to $500, the opportunity to thieve was great. The criminals that I caught were smart and only claimed between $80 and $150 at a time. They would hand over the gift card with a proof of purchase and take off with the cash. The illegal part comes in when the criminal hands over a forged receipt with a fake activation code and incorrect information on the activation fee.

My current file, which I began working on a month earlier, revealed a tricky new twist. The smarter criminals were just taking the forged activation codes and finding a way to manipulate the system to allow them to activate the cards. A lot of computer code and cracking was involved. As one of my IT friends had explained: Hackers are good, Crackers are bad. Hackers seek to point out back doors and weak points in code; Crackers seek to exploit these breaks for their own gain. The Crackers were finding a way to activate the gift cards, transfer the money to an online account to purchase items, or just reload their online payment accounts. The systems were catching on within 20 minutes of fraudulent activity, so the thieves had to cover their tracks quickly. They were forced to virtually launder the money. Many were funneling the money through innocuous websites that likely had no idea that their pages were being used for such nefarious activities.

The majority of the transactions were run through the RF server. Yes, the popular and often imitated RF server had been used in all of this. The first, of now many, self-service web-hosting companies was Roman's Forum, now abbreviated to RF. The founder, Roman, who had started out by offering up his free webpage codes in online forums, was just trying to be helpful and pass the time while he was bored at his desk job. He finally got funding and launched the WYSIWYG platform that allows just about anyone to sign up and start a website for free, with advanced design and analytics options for a monthly subscription fee. He was a genius and now WordPress, Squarespace, Wix, and all of the others in the market were trying to copy the model.

The one item that often brought the founder, Roman, praise was that he headquartered his company in Philadelphia. He brought tech jobs to the city and managed to staunch the flow of the post-graduate brain-drain from Philadelphia colleges and universities.

The downside is that this guy, Roman, was that he is the same one that I referenced earlier. That's right, in this case, all roads lead back to Avila. My latest case involved a cracker who was funneling laundered money through Roman's Forum. I had been avoiding direct and even indirect interaction for a while. The first few instances involved sloppy criminals and a multitude of websites that didn't go through the RF server.

My latest file was on a criminal that had found a way to massage and manipulate the RF server so that he had a longer time window to launder his digital money. In my mind, this was a stupid criminal because he was using the same paths over and over again. It was as if he wanted to get caught. Nevertheless, this also meant that I had to seek the cooperation of Roman's Forum to be able to provide evidence on the user and close the case. *Was there a deeper conspiracy at hand? Did this criminal somehow know of my weak spot, my aversion? Perhaps they were smarter than I thought.*

My headache was starting to dig in. I rubbed my head to try and convince it to stop hurting.

At the end of that long Monday, I felt that I had made a significant accomplishment. I was one fifth through that week that would get more difficult every day as the book launch approached. My sanity was still mostly intact and I had been fairly productive at work in spite of my Tourettic habit of pitying myself and ruminating on my hatred of Avila. After a good workout, a lousy dinner, and a mind-numbing hour of television, I was ready for sleep. I had taken an over-the-counter sleep aid and washed it down with some water, fresh and fluoridated.

Against my better judgment, I continued to watch TV. I thought that once the pill kicked in, I could really exhaust myself if I fought the urge to sleep. Yes, I do tend to follow the advice that I give myself, even if it makes no sense.

My eyes lolled between the TV screen and the empty walls of my apartment. As my thoughts wandered from the weak plot line of the show and began to focus on my immediate surroundings, I became fixed on thoughts of my apartment. The walls were empty and bare, as would be expected of any young bachelor.

I wasn't that young anymore, though. There were pockets of furniture between wide expanses of open floors. There was a wasteland, a wilderness, of empty space in the apartment where dust clumps would form and stick to the floorboards. I hadn't ever really settled in, but I was somehow ingrained to this threadbare space. I could always excuse the appearance by giving a line about consumerism and trying to appear as though I was deliberately keeping my space clean and my possessions to a minimum. Really, I was just too apathetic and lazy to make a solid decision. I was too caught in my own past to ever really settle in, but I was also too committed in my hope for a happy future to accept that I needed a massive change in my life.

I should have been living out in Manayunk, but instead I stayed in the heart of the city. I should have been living the life that the rest of my generation was so keen to post and share with ease. But I was trapped, I was shut-off, and I couldn't stop lying to myself. It was just so easy at that point to continue the ruse.

The show ended and the blaring theme of the news report caught my attention. I snapped back to reality and looked at the TV, forgetting all self-pitying thoughts of my inner turmoil being manifested in my undecorated apartment.

As the nightly news faded into comedy re-runs, I heard my cell phone buzz. From the comfort of my couch, I looked around to see where I had left it in the apartment. There was a soft glow from the kitchen and I heard the buzz again. I calculated the effort required to stand up and walk the few feet to the kitchen counter. It seemed an insurmountable feat at the time. My muscles and joints were succumbing to the effects of the sleeping pill; I was weighted down with chemical lead in my veins.

After the second distinct buzz there was silence. In that silence, I contemplated my pathetic position of being too lazy to get up and answer my own phone. I bullied myself into standing and made the three-second journey to the other side of my apartment. I palmed the phone and swiped to access my home screen. The compact and innocuous yellow icon that led to my text messages had a bright red circle in the upper right-hand corner with the number "2" on it. This indicated that I had not one, but two messages awaiting my response. The small joys of lonely adulthood include getting two text messages on a weeknight. *Hooray!* I thought in my exhausted state.

I opened up the messages, both were from Nick. My good ole buddy Nick who never kept in touch, or called, or made plans to get drinks, or offered a spare Phillies ticket, or made any attempt to contact me unless Avila was involved. We had been great friends. During the time that Avila and I were together we were "couple-friends" with Nick and his then-girlfriend. Nick had been a very chill guy and was dating one of Avila's good friends. We grouped together at parties, we went on double dates, the girls chatted in the kitchen while Nick and I watched the Birds on Sunday nights. It was a cozy view of domesticated life and I suspect that Nick and I would have remained closer if his then-girlfriend, now wife, Claudette, hadn't sided with Avila. I lost the girl and the associated friends in the split, but at least I got to keep the city.

After it all ended, Avila left town, but Claudette and Nick stayed loyal to her. Nick had sent me text messages for a while asking how I was and tried to make an effort, as though he wasn't completely whipped by Claudette.

When Avila's novels were released, he would send an email asking how I had been and giving some perfunctory life updates. Within one or two responses, he would usually steer the conversation to Avila and the latest book. Nick was aware of the trend that I had detected in her novels, I had told him my theory as the relationship was imploding. While he may have been elusive and absent as a friend most of the time, he did remain true to me in one aspect. Nick would read Avila's novels, as Claudette would expect him to, but he would keep an eye out for any romantic references. Nick would send me chunks of text with the simple note: "don't know if this means you or not, but figured you would be curious."

He actually kept the same text in his emails with each subsequent release. I began to suspect that he was just copying and pasting from one email to the next. It was a CRTL-ALT-Friendship, but he did help me through the anguish I was feeling. I could picture him making notes in the margins and dog-earring pages so that he could reference them again as he peered over and copied one sentence at a time into his emails. How dedicated he must have been to the task. Perhaps he had been a better friend to me in all of this than anyone else, perhaps he had been better to me than I had been to myself.

Unfortunately, none of the passages that he sent meant much to me. I had read them through quickly, acting as though I didn't care. Later, I would meticulously study the text in the insomnia hours that followed. As you might have suspected when Avila's books went silent, so did Nick.

That evening his simple messages of, "Hey man" and then "How have you been?" were like the sound of an expected drumbeat. It felt like the tension released as the Tchaikovsky cannons were fired. I expected it. I knew it was coming, but it still rattled me each time and was followed by the period of familiar unease. *What if he stumbled across the passages written about me this time?*

As I stared at the text messages, I thought back to the most haunting passages he had sent me yet. I couldn't see myself in any of them. I tried to force myself into the descriptions, but it never worked. Avila hadn't written me in, *yet*. But some of her words started to get under my skin. I realized what true darkness was within her and wondered at how she must have transformed, transmorphed into some kind of twisted woman. Like this one:

'My long strands, gray beneath, but died brown then black then auburn, will cling to the small hairs on your arms, stick in the

crook of your elbow like spider-webs and creep you out each and every time one slithers from the baseboards and up your body."

-Scarlett Moore and the Missing Volcano

So weird, right? Or this one:

"Does the orange and freshly oxygenated blood on my hands appease you? Should I mutilate myself some more? Should I scratch through another layer of skin on my palms and grind them into the gravel to be worthy of your touch?"

-Scarlett Moore and the Embargo of Eden

The plots of the Scarlett Moore novels became progressively darker. The descriptions were becoming more eerie and warped. Was Avila crumbling under the pressure? Was it the result of something dark planted within her that was starting to take root? Were the grotesque depictions a result of her desire to seek retribution on me? It had occurred to me that she may have just enjoyed writing in that style, but that left my ego unappeased.

I locked my phone without responding to Nick and placed it face-down on the kitchen counter where it had been idling. I sauntered back to the couch trying to convince myself that I wasn't distracted by the memory of the dark passages Avila had penned and Nick had transcribed. I watched the remainder of a B-rated sitcom rerun that barely managed to keep my attention.

I felt the groggy haze of the sleeping pill starting to take hold, even though my mind was wildly active. Each synapse and cognitive function tried to pull up those selected passages and work at deciphering them again. My memory was searching for some previously undiscovered clue, some hint as to the revenge Avila was undoubtedly plotting against me.

The show ended and I turned the television off. I was out-of-whack and so desperately wanted this mania to end, but I could see no way out of it now. I silently hoped for a night of dreamless sleep as I picked up my cell phone on the way to my bedroom. As my routine dictated, I set my phone to be charged, checked my alarm, and shuffled into the bathroom to brush my teeth and wash my face. I ran through the motions quickly and without thought, but my mind was still active. The servers in my 1,000-computer brain were whirring, spinning, and just getting started for the night.

As I settled into bed, I tried to focus on my denial.

Maybe she'll never write me in. Perhaps she had written it all out in some other story but refused to publish that work. Or perhaps she has cut out and braided each line into a thick rope that she will use to hang me.

Avila would find that appropriate. The monstrous vision of Avila I had constructed in my mind was capable of that. Based on her last novel, that dark matter in her mind had exploded outward. I wouldn't put it past her now. She was a femme fatale with creative license, and she was sharpening her pen just for me.

After a restless evening I climbed out of my own bed and started my morning routine. A quick shower, then a shave. It was slightly more painful because I had an extra day's worth of stubble on my chin. I recall the stubborn burn of the blade as it tugged, and pulled, and finally cut the short hairs on my jaw line. Like everything that week, it was drawn-out and painful.

I settled in at my desk, with a fresh cup of coffee, and flipped through my usual links to check the news, log in to the requisite systems, and then finally to review the flags for any fraudulent activity. Like a bright and shining star, there was another transaction by this latest fraudster, he went by the handle: Traveler. Usually, he opted for some derivation of the word in his moniker: +R@v3l3r, or T®a<ele®, or some mixture of symbols and letters that spelled out the same word: Traveler.

This guy was actually very good at what he was doing. He had once again enabled a gift card with a fake activation code, found a way to arbitrage the currency through several websites, and was off with the money in 5 minutes. Once again, all of the sites were hosted through Roman's Forum and it appeared that he had used the same websites multiple times.

I shook my head at that last detail. I wanted to respect this man for his ingenuity. If I could respect him and his criminal acuity then I could think like him, get in his head, and try to predict his next move. But I couldn't respect how lazy he was. *Was he trying to get caught?* It is an established fact within the cracking world that you don't use the same path more than once, and here this Traveler was flaunting his indifference to even his own criminal code. Did he have no respect for anything?

I might have called out to my desk-mate to say, "can you believe this guy?" or some similar remark. But, my most recent neighbor had been transferred to Pittsburgh and the cube next to mine was starkly empty. The carpets were beige, the cubicle walls were beige, and even the ambient noises gave off an overall mood of beige.

The office was quiet and everyone was keen to keep their heads down and get their work done. Except for the din of office white noise, there was no noise to catch my attention away from my thoughts. What I recall most about that week was the silence, the rattling and overwhelming silence from the real world. I was left to contend with the voices in my head far too often. Usually, this was great for me, but that week it was a torture. The isolation made things worse.

With this latest transaction, Traveler was up to over $76,000 in laundered funds. I needed to act quickly before he hit a major milestone number, like $100,000, and disappear into the refuge of an island nation with no extradition laws.

I went through the process of cataloging the transaction and added it to a report I had already started. The additional details confirmed the pattern, the laundering process, and that the Traveler (I had to refer to him as "the suspect" in the report for official purposes) would likely do this several more times before taking off with the money. My number one recommendation was to ask Roman's Forum for access to their logs so that we could accurately verify the identity of the suspect. We had the I.P. addresses that were used to access the funds, but most crackers were able to mask their I.P. address, so it did us little good. We needed the logs from RF to confirm the final destination of the funds and trace that back to the actual identity and location of the Traveler. He might not even be within Philadelphia city limits. This guy could be operating out of a basement in Utah. He could in fact be a world traveler. We couldn't know until we found the end of that trail.

I debated disclosing my connection with Roman in the report. Each time I began to type out the explanation, it seemed more and more ridiculous.

"We have a past lover in common…"

"He dated my ex-girlfriend before I did…"

"I can only assume that he knows who I am and holds an unwarranted animosity towards me…"

"He may not even know who I am, but I know who he is and it could get weird…"

I deleted each thought before it was completed. No need to make any mention of it at all. I had no evidence to suggest that Roman Trecki was knowingly abetting criminal activity on his server. He likely didn't know the day-to-day minutia of each user and link accessed. There was no plausible reason for me to implicate him and no grounds for it. I wasn't so out of whack over Avila that I would knowingly incriminate an innocent man.

I didn't want my fear over a perceived bias to mask any potential criminal activity. I was good at my job and was set against letting Avila have a hold over me at work as well. I needed to start building up a firewall against her in my mind. She may be ramming the gates of my life with her forthcoming novel, but I had to keep my workplace the bastion of sanity and professionalism. At least, those were my best intentions.

I finished my report and shot it over to my Director via email. Like a good agent, I awaited his approval on my proposed plan of action.

After a few minutes, I performed the habitual motion. The ritualistic check. From the Facebook homepage it was easy to navigate. The past searches populated the instant I typed the letter "A."

The Avila Chase fan page always displayed first on the list. The picture was unchanged; Avila was laughing with a sly smile. Perhaps it was a genuine candid, but likely it was a staged photo. By the look of the background, she was at some event.

The second result was her actual personal page. The bright blue check mark next to her name indicated that it was her official page and genuinely belonged to her. I clicked and saw the same message that I had seen each time I had checked in the previous years. "This user's profile has been disabled. Please check back later."

I knew that if she really disabled her account that her personal profile wouldn't have populated at all in the search. Had she blocked me perhaps? Maybe she had such a following on social media that she could retain her personal profile, but still allow it to appear disabled to those she wasn't friends with.

I clicked the bright red "X" in the top corner of the internet browser window and hurriedly clicked onto anything else. An old tax file popped up on my screen.

What did that famous statesman, so well-known in Philadelphia, once say? "Nothing in life is certain except for death and taxes." Perhaps Ben Franklin omitted heartache from his list because he never knew Avila Chase.

The cover design for Scarlett: Avenged had been revealed earlier that summer with an alternate design. The primary cover art was the staring, cold eyes of Avila, likely used because she herself strongly resembled the written description of Scarlett. This was the image that I found myself constantly confronting throughout the city. Each day it was as though she was brow-beating me into a state of deranged paranoia.

The alternate design, probably what she and her publishing team expected would be used for the inevitable movie poster, didn't offer me much relief. The second design was a graphic of the Hindu god, Kali. The blue-skinned figure with multiple arms was facing away from the viewer and appeared to have long and flowing red hair, instead of the traditionally depicted black hair. As if I hadn't pictured, on multiple occasions, Avila coming after me with her animal hands trying to claw out my eyes and smother me with the weight of her fury. The alternate design was terrifying to me on so many new levels.

When I stepped out of the building for lunch that Tuesday afternoon, I was sick of my poor self-control and inability to focus. It was the worst possible week for an Avila Chase distraction, I wanted to catch the Traveler. I was thinking of his odd actions and potential motives as I strolled a block or so to reach my favorite spot for lunch. The air was clean and temperate. I could breathe easily and enjoyed seeing the streets of the city busy with other 9-to-5-ers resting on ledges and benches to enjoy their lunches.

I quickened my pace and managed to avoid slipping on the grease spots in the street as I jaywalked to the best spot for lunch in town. This place was an alley featuring a bank of food trucks that offered every kind of cuisine. They were busy that day, as each truck had a decent line for food.

There were medical professionals in mint green scrubs, chatting amongst themselves; an endless sea of pens, and clips, and id badges pouring out of their top breast pockets. There were women in heels and binding professional ensembles that made me think that they must be uncomfortable. There were other men in suits who had eschewed their blazers as they stood in line, they held them over their shoulders with one hand. A pose that they had likely seen in a catalog.

It was a perfect Philadelphian afternoon. People were out and about; the city was alive and bustling. Each person was moving like a blood cell in an intricate system, keeping the pulse of the city beating.

Oh, Philadelphia. The city that will remain loyal to you, so long as you remain loyal to it. It was a close family-member that was always there. It was the warm embrace that I felt every time I caught the sunset refracting off the Cira Center. It was the romanticized notions that stirred up as I passed the outdated long-boats at Penn's Landing. If I could only keep one thing in my relationship with Avila, I'm glad that I kept this city.

I went to my favorite Chinese food truck and put in an order of sesame chicken and lo mein with a Coke. It was a five-dollar deal that you just couldn't beat. As I dawdled while my order was prepared, I wondered about how the Traveler might be maneuvering. I wandered a few feet as I ran through the information on the case in my mind. I stopped in front of a newsstand and leaned against the brick wall that was behind me. Once I had cycled through the clues mentally, I entertained myself by perusing the headlines in front of me.

One particular item caught my eye. I saw the intricate Kali/Scarlett design on the cover of *Philadelphia Magazine*. The story headline revealed that an interview with her was, in fact, the premier editorial for that month.

I picked up the magazine without even thinking and flipped through to the article. I tried to scan quickly, as though I was just a casual customer considering a purchase. I knew that I couldn't buy the magazine, though. It would be another means of torture to remind myself of my imminent doom. I found the interview.

The feature took up five pages, three of text and two of images. Avila was featured in profile in full make-up and hair blown-out. She was styled to look so glamorous. *How could they all not see how devious she was? How could people not see how hell-bent she was on destroying any man who dared to not love her forever?* I could see her as the man-eater that she was, though. I flipped through her answers quickly.

The interview was by the lead entertainment and events editor for the magazine, Dan Dorr, whose initials are listed as "DD" for reference:

DD: Avila, your work is technically categorized as science fiction because Scarlett focuses on out-of-this world phenomenon. But each novel has an underlying message. What is the main focus for Scarlett: Avenged?

AC: Scarlett may be investigating paranormal activities, but it is always human errors that bring her back into this world. I wanted to focus on an issue that is important not just to women, but to society. We can't just say this is a woman's issue anymore, it's a human issue. Through Scarlett I can bring this problem to the forefront of our consciousness and hopefully spur change.

DD: And what inspired this specific message? This is your most outspoken work to date.

AC: What inspires anything? A personal connection, an experience that shifted my world view. It has taken some time to put my head around it, but I can see clearly that I need to take action and bring this to light.

My stomach began to churn. Was this it? Was this the moment when she would reveal me as the negative focal point, the demon waiting in the wings, that had driven her creativity and success? I wasn't reading anymore. I was scanning ferociously. There were some references to Calcutta and a trip to Nepal. Blah, blah, blah.

Then, at the end of the interview was an excerpt from the novel. Out of place and out of context, I had no way to tell for sure what it referred to, but it left me spooked:

I envision your first punching me, my fist punching you. My head slamming into your face, my oversized and unadorned forehead causing your front teeth to rip and pull from their gums. And each time, I see you holding up a bloody tooth, slimy with saliva. Your hand receives the blood as well, but the pulp of your teeth are not pink or even red like the fluids spilling from the sucking hole in your mouth. No, the pulp of your teeth, the fleshy matter that had once held it in, is like a thick patch of seaweeds. Flowing and breathing in the air, roots as white as your tooth, the remainder of the pulp is black. Inky black like an octopus, a slippery squeezing suffocating octopus. It's just like you, that is what you are.
-Scarlett: Avenged

At the sight of those words my hands twitched, releasing the magazine, letting it fall onto the grimy sidewalk. I picked it up quickly, crushing it in my hands. I tried to casually place it back on shelf. The pages were bent and crumpled. I couldn't steady myself or keep my hands from making a mess. The newspaper stand owner called out to me, "Stop fooling around and buy it already!" The men and women nearby looked at me with disdain. I was the interrupter of the idyllic peace they were enjoying as they waited for their fast food. I was the crazy man, crouched on the ground, fumbling for papers, reminding them how fragile sanity can be.

I couldn't find the words in my throat to answer. I

shook my head and wobbled away. I almost forgot my lunch order, but happened to pause to catch my breath as I heard my name called out in a heavy accent. I felt as though I was a wanted criminal, on the run, hiding in plain sight, and my cover was just blown by a clear and crisp wanted photo. Was everyone around me looking at me because I was sweating profusely, even though the weather was lovely? Were they worried that I was sick? Or perhaps, my secret was not so secret at all? Could there be some way for people to know my connection to Avila? Some kind of literary gossip scene that would clearly point the finger at me as the inspiration of her latest villain, her greatest villain yet based on the words in her interview?

Was the older woman, peering at me over the top of her fuchsia glasses, with her brightly dyed auburn hair, judging me? Did she know my secret? Was she reading my thoughts? Did she know my sins just by taking one look at me?

I wasn't even hungry anymore, but I brought my lunch back to my desk. I began to compulsively check online one more time. This time I typed in my own name and found no connections to Avila Chase on the first three pages of the Google Search Engine Results. Thank goodness for that.

I ate my lunch in silence. I could have gone into the breakroom and struck up a conversation with any person passing by, but I elected my solitude. When it came time to open up my fortune cookie, I couldn't do it. I had tempted fate enough for one day. Besides, I had an overwhelming feeling that the tiny slip of paper would have lottery numbers to match Avila's birthday and that the fortune would read: "*Scarlett: Avenged*, by Philadelphia's daughter Avila Chase available this Friday!"

Avila was indeed my future; I was being pushed towards that fate every second.

"Good work, Hobbertson."

Those three words were my salvation on that Tuesday. They brought me out of my post-lunch hated-fueled panic.

My Director had called me into his office. He was well into his fifties with a paunch that constantly tugged at his shirts, the fibers appearing more and more tired with every second that passed. He was a good man. I will stand by that assessment to this day. Randy Knight is a good man. A wife and three kids with a McMansion out in Yardley, he was the mild-mannered and even-tempered FBI Director that you would hope to see. Not so driven by ambition as to be ruthless, but not so aimless as to sit by idly without taking action.

"Thank you, sir." I accepted my praise standing, watching Knight as he put the file containing my report back down onto his desk.

"Make contact with this Forums website today if you can. If your suspect is moving fast, he may wrap things up by this weekend. Why not? Am I right?"

"Yes, sir. Their headquarters are actually adjacent to City Hall, so I planned to drop in tomorrow morning before coming into the office."

"Great. Just in case they aren't as open and willing to help, have the warrant ready. These tech companies act so touchy when we ask for help. We want to catch criminals; why are we being treated like the bad guys because we are asking for specific information?" Knight shrugged and shook his head; it was clear that he was censoring a much longer diatribe that was still running through his mind.

I agreed with each word he said, nodding along as he spoke.

"What am I telling you this for? You know it!" He patted the folder as though it were a small and precocious child. Knight had that odd habit. "Alright, Hobbertson, good work." I gave a curt nod and slipped out of his office.

I had never pictured myself as a 'yes-man' or a

'company-man.' But I did find comfort in being told that I was doing good work, in having my efforts recognized. I had been in an existential funk after things ended with Avila. I had spent years trying to get over her and I had found that the most effective method was to channel my energy into my work. That week I was experiencing the clawing effects of a relapse. Working hard and performing at my job kept me focused and grounded. It reminded me that I was one of the good guys, no matter what Avila thought or wrote about me.

I sat back in my chair and dialed the main number of RF. After an onerous phone tree and some hipster wait music, I finally spoke with a receptionist. She informed me politely that Mr. Trecki was absolutely booked and couldn't take any appointments. Once I clarified who I was and the reason for my meeting request she put me on hold. I felt a surge of power knowing that my title: "Special Agent" and employer: "The Federal Bureau of Investigation" aka "The Federal Bureau of Look At My Badge, Get Out Of My Way" would clear a path for me. I tried not to become addicted to that feeling, because it can be intoxicating. But I enjoyed that sensation of power and control as the receptionist took me off of hold and informed me that Mr. Trecki would be able to meet with me first thing the following morning.

"Thank you, I will be in at 9 am," I said politely, as though I hadn't just played the trump-card in this situation.

"Excellent. We look forward to seeing you then." The receptionist cut the line after her overly cheery salutation. In that moment, I felt good. I felt in control. I knew that I had no ability to influence Avila, to persuade her to cease her mental torture, but I sure could get a lowly receptionist to jump at my command. That did feel good.

While I would have reclined at my desk for an extended period and basked in the glory of a job-well-done, I had plans that evening. I had plans every Tuesday evening. It was 10k Tuesday. I was part of the local run-club that would meet up and run through the city. We would meet at Philadelphia Runner at 16th and Sansom and head for the Schuylkill River Park, then follow that path up to the Art Museum. Some of the faster runners would add the steps to their run, after looping around to the front while waiting for the slower runners to catch-up, before heading down the parkway to Logan Square and back to the run-shop. Of course, we had to have drinks afterwards. We were young and upwardly mobile millennials. We would do just about anything that seemed like an accomplishment if it meant we could go drinking afterwards.

While we had discussed varying our run route and trying a different bar each week, we usually settled into the same route and almost always ended up at The Happy Rooster.

That week was no different. I left work at 5pm sharp. I had informed Knight of my weekly run-routine and he approved heartily. He would occasionally come up to my desk at 4:45 pm on Tuesdays and make small talk just so he could say, "Oh, would you look at the time. You've gotta get going if you want to make your run club."

I couldn't tell if he was being sincere or if he just wanted to feel somehow included. I had invited him to join us once or twice. He never took me up on the offer. For a man with a sedentary lifestyle, I think just saying the word "run" got his heart rate elevated for the recommended 30 minutes.

That week I had my computer shut down and my desk cleaned right on time. I slipped out quietly and headed home. Most nights I would stay until 6:30 or 7:00 pm with the other agents. I didn't sense any animosity from them because of my weekly indulgence, but I still didn't try to make a big thing of it. I waved to Director Knight as he came out of his office and caught my eye.

After a brisk walk home and a change into my running clothes, I grabbed a banana and a cool bottle of water, then headed to meet the group. My previous routine had consisted of running only on the weekends. About a year earlier, I had inadvertently run into this club. I came up behind a large group of people, most going at a steady pace. I had intended to go around them, but I ended up sticking with them until they ended their run. I started talking to a few of the club members and joined up.

I didn't have much social interaction outside of the Bureau. It was hard to find people that could relate to our line of work and hours. But the run club was great. Most people didn't share what they did for work and that was just fine by me. The only one who knew what I did was Justin, he was the organizer of the group. He was a cool guy and he always had great advice for improving my technique. I don't take constructive criticism very well, but his unsolicited suggestions actually helped me cut my half marathon time down by 10 minutes.

Each week we would all discuss different running gear, or training methods. Some would sign up to do fun-runs together, but most of the group was focused on The Broad Street Run and then the Philadelphia Marathon.

As I approached the run shop, there were already a few of the club members loitering around. I was welcomed heartily by Justin, our de facto leader. He was short, bearded, and always up for making others laugh. I assumed that he was a drama teacher of some kind when we first met, but because of our connection via social media, I did know that he was a graphic designer.

When the weather was beautiful, as it was that day, we usually saw an up-tick in group membership. Most of the die-hards persisted through the winter and they comprised the core group. I was one of the core-group.

Justin and his fiancé, Jasmine, were talking to a woman who had joined us for the weekly run a few times throughout the summer. She was timid, and shy, and clearly was just starting to get into shape. I rolled my eyes. *Wasn't this a group for serious runners?*

A few of the other core group members approached: Rod, Tom, and a guy that I was fairly sure went by Tiger. I couldn't be sure, when he had first introduced himself a year earlier it really sounded like he said, "My name is Tiger." I didn't want to offend him and react in a rude way so I accepted this. And then I never felt that it was the right time to ask him his name again.

After another 10 or so minutes of chatting about the weather and hearing about the status of Rod's shin-splints, some new faces joined the group. A few were a little familiar, others I had never seen before. This was going to be a big group, which made Justin happy. He would have a larger audience to try his latest jokes on.

We took off at 6:00 sharp. I heard the dissonant chirps of the different tracking watches beeping as the group members activated their devices. My stamina had improved since joining the club. In addition to my other weekly workouts to stay in shape for work, I was one of the out-in-front runners, keeping stride with Justin and Tom. I had even been able to start running the steps, a solid sign that I was no slow-poke.

We made it up to the third tier of steps on the Art Museum before returning to the street to join the rest of the group. It felt great to do something that my body was just good at doing. I was strong. I had always been strong and in shape, but on that afternoon, I could feel that I was really lean, healthy, and fit.

The group finished up by 6:50 pm, the leaders were already stretching and chatting as the stragglers came in. Justin had been a good leader in that he insisted on everyone meeting up again when we finished and not letting the slower folks in the club feel left out. I would have been happy to head straight to the bar instead of waiting, but everyone else waited, so I did too. Apparently, Jasmine had taken the initiative to work out a deal with the bar owner so that we could enjoy some discounted appetizers each week. We were regulars and we could use this as a selling point to encourage people to join the group. The restaurant made more off us this way; it was a win-win.

We sauntered into The Happy Rooster and found our usual corner. I usually would have ordered my standard Yuengling, but the more health-conscious members of the club always opted for the gluten-free option. I caved to peer-pressure (or rather beer-pressure) and went with that too. It didn't taste too bad and it made that beer special. *I only drink gluten-free beer when I'm with my running buddies.* I made a meme of myself, *I don't always drink gluten-free beer, but when I do it's because I've just run 10k.*

I spent the early part of that evening talking with Jasmine who was happy to share the details of the latest wedding plans she was working on with Justin. Justin was talking with the newer runners. I probably should have been doing that too. I had a million little excuses not to, that really added up to the fact that I just didn't want to make small-talk.

I finished my beer and enjoyed the chips and spinach dip that I split with Rod. At an appropriate hour, I made my way to the door. I said my good-byes and "see ya next week" to the members of our group that I was standing closest to. I was heading towards the front door, which happened to be where Justin was standing. I waved good-bye, not wanting to interrupt the conversation he was having with one of the girls that was new to our group. I still don't know her name, she only showed up once or twice after that week.

As I passed Justin called out, "Hey man!"

"Good run today. See ya next week!" I waved and continued walking.

"Wait, wait," he beckoned me over. Justin was always a gregarious fellow; he was overly friendly and social even when sober. After two beers, he was everyone's best friend.

"I barely got to catch up with you," he waved me over with his free hand, the nearly empty beer bottle occupying the other.

"Eh, not much to report. Felt good today, I can feel my mile-splits getting faster."

"That's great, you're gonna need that to rank in your age group next year at Broad Street."

I shrugged off the competitive dare he was making, hoping that if I seemed nonchalant that I would protect my ego if I didn't rank. I also knew I had the better part of a year ahead to improve, or injure myself. "Eh, we'll see. I want to enjoy the experience of the run. I'm not going out for a ranking."

"Yeah, ok." Justin made a face suggesting that he was onto my game. His closely trimmed beard exacerbated his expressions. You might have expected it to mask his emotion, but it seems to have grown onto him. The beard latched into his nerve endings and became an extension of his expressive gestures. At this point the new girl to our group had been pulled into a conversation with Jasmine about her running tights, they were apparently very fashionable.

"Well, you're definitely gonna rank, so you don't have to sweat it." I figured complimenting Justin would make him happy in his intoxicated state and perhaps give me the chance to leave.

"Ah man. You never know," he shrugged. "But hey, this is a big week for you. You holding up okay?"

His comment perplexed me and rendered me speechless. The first thought that ran through my mind was that he knew about Traveler. *How could he know about the case? Did he know who the Traveler was?*

Then, it hit me. It was just like the terrifying moment in a film when you see the serial killer in a flash of lightning before the theatre is engrossed in total darkness. I realized what he meant by his flippant comment: *Avila.* I furrowed my brow and pursed my lips. My shoulders were raised; my hands went into my pockets. I was in a defensive position.

"Uh, what do you mean?" My immediate reaction was to play dumb, to pretend that my mind hadn't quickly riddled out the meaning.

"You know," Justin gestured with his hand, as though his quick motions were a foreign sign language for me to riddle out.

I shook my head. I wasn't going to say it. I was scared silent that he was about to bring her up.

"You know, your old lady," Justin rested his gesticulating hand on my shoulder. "I know that this has gotta be a tough week on you. The posters are everywhere. I want you to know, me and Jasmine, we're here for you man."

I shook my head. I knew I should have never accepted his friend request, but I didn't have many genuine friends at the time. Actually, I didn't have any genuine friends. He would have seen old photos from parties that I hadn't bothered to un-tag. He would have easily done the mental math to figure out that in another life, I was once the love interest of Avila Chase. I thought that I had been making a good connection with the run club. In that moment though, it was stained like a purloined sack of cash with a dye bomb. I'll have to quit the club. *I'll have to block Justin on Facebook. I'll have to finally un-tag those photos, and change my name, and leave the country.*

"Yeah, thanks." My social abilities shut down at the mention of her. Another flash of lightning in my mind. She, the elusive serial killer of my imagination, was now closer. She was coming for me. She was looming in the darkness ready to sink her knife into my stomach. "Uh, I really gotta get going man. I have an early day tomorrow."

"Alright, alright," Justin put his arms over his head, showing his surrender. "But you call if you need me. I got you man!" He flashed his charismatic smile and I gave a subdued smirk in return. The rational part of my brain kept telling me to keep my cool. *He was just trying to be a friend; I could use one right now.* The emotional side of my brain kept screaming to be heard, *screw you Avila, you ruin everything!*

I walked home briskly, feeling a strange paranoia. I had seen in each face that I passed, the knowing glance; I was exposed and my deepest fears had been laid bare. I heard footsteps behind me. They were almost rhythmic: *Av-ila. Av-ila. Av-ila.* The syllables of her name called out in a pattern. At least that is what they sounded like. Perhaps they could have been: *Trav-eler. Trav-eler. Trav-eler.* I tried to keep my head down, ducking eye contact, and walking faster with each step. The pattern kept repeating, but I could hear those steps getting closer and closer. The person making these sounds was right behind me.

My pace quickened as I almost broke out into a run back to my apartment. I refused to look behind me as I fumbled with the keys and let myself into the building. The person who had been so close behind me surely had no control over the sounds of their steps. My mind had planted those words there. *Av-ila. Av-ila. Av-ila.*

I had somehow mapped the posters with Avila's seeing eyes and avoided them along my route. She was an intricate bundle of gray coated wires; each alive with electric current and ready to shock you. Her eyes would only remind me of that. I ran up the stairs to my apartment, too agitated to take the calm and even-paced elevator.

I kicked off my sneakers and tried to take a few calming deep breathes, but I felt my chest tighten and my trachea pinch with each attempt. I quickly unscrewed the top of a water bottle. I was squeezing it so tightly in my hand that water spilled out all over me. I took a heavy swig before placing the bottle down on the counter and starting the process of cleaning up my mess. The last thing I needed was to slip and fall on a small puddle in my own kitchen and give myself a concussion.

After I had cleaned up the kitchen and finished the rest of the bottle of water, I felt significantly calmer. I had already begun to chastise myself for how silly I had been.

Would I let my own ego get in the way of my mental calm? What Justin said was the actual truth, it was a rough week for me. *Why was I so determined to deny her?* I didn't have to do it often, but telling people I didn't know her was easy now. I told that lie often enough to make Peter look like a loyal Apostle. I didn't want to just be "Avila's ex" forever, but it was the most present part of my identity. I didn't know how to distance myself from it. I began to finally ruminate of the true source of my worry. *What if she did write me in? What if it is horrible? What if it is true, and I have to face that I am no more than a common villain, an expendable character?*

I refused to turn on the television. I had tried to distract myself with it the night before without much luck. I went to bed and concentrated on the hairline cracks in the plaster ceiling above me. I tried to focus on my joints, sore and tired from the run. I went about the task of boring myself so that I could fall, and stay, asleep.

In the first dream that evening, I found myself in a living room of an unfamiliar apartment, the sounds of typing and chewing were the only things I could hear at first. This dream was so vivid, I could have sworn I had been transported in time and space to a moment in another reality. Given the all-encompassing nature of my thoughts that week, it should have been no surprise that the person I saw in this dream was Avila.

She sat alone with her computer and her thoughts. I can still picture her in that room: sitting at her desk, clacking away at the keyboard, really digging into me with her latest lines. She was blaring some pissed-chic pop or maybe it was the tantrum of a female rock-and-roller through the thin speakers of her desktop. I could see the fine details of those fiery red locks of hers, large voluminous waves moving like the tide as her head bobbed along to the beat. A paragraph finished, an indictment against me, and just in time for the hook of the song. I could see her, waving her finger at a picture of me as if to say "I told you not to mess with me."

Could she be this worked up so many years after the fact? Could this all just be in my head? I sure hoped so.

> *Do you have squeamish nightmares and call out to your mommy in the pitch black of our old bedroom, now yours alone? Do you watch those scary scenes in your mind of my nipples morphing into oversized and obese tardigrades, awakened and scurrying over to you, so that they feast on the skin cells that you shed unconsciously?*
>
> *-Scarlett Moore and the Hopeless Case of the Poltergeist*

Wednesday started after another bad night of sleep. It left a darkness just beneath my eyes that highlighted every toss, turn, and nightmare. I dressed in a full suit: black on black with a crisp white button-down and blue-knitted tie. As I made the knot in the tie, it reminded me of the vision of Avila from the night before last, the lines of text tied into a rope. I shivered at the thought.

I dressed for my meeting with Roman, knowing that I needed to secure the necessary access to the web logs in order to file an arrest warrant for the Traveler. He was within my reach, almost too quickly.

I tried to override each thought of jealousy that I once felt toward Roman as I prepared. I began to reason with myself that even if he and Avila were together, it would actually be a blessing to me. Not only would it vindicate me, but I certainly would not want to be with her either. I tried to be the rational adult that was able to successfully investigate and conclude cases. I needed to be the professional version of myself that morning. I could afford no slip-ups as the result of my personal pains.

When clearing my mind that morning, I started to realize that, for as much as I had been focused on his role in the dissolution of my relationship with Avila, I didn't know much about Roman at all. I had only a vague mental image of this man who was the acid that etched and carved through the tenuous fibers of what had at one time been a fragile and blossoming love.

After much delay, bordering on incompetence really, I made my way to the RF headquarters in a trendy corner of the old Wannamaker building. I evaded this interaction for months because of my personal aversion to the man. And it was during that fated week that we were finally thrust into the same time and space.

I navigated past the confused tourists funneling out of Suburban Station, the gawkers who stopped to photograph City Hall, and shouldered my way through the brass-lined revolving door and over to the elevators.

As I entered the offices of Roman's Forum, Inc. (RF), I was surprised at the efficient use of space. For what was most certainly a small square footage, the offices looked spacious. It was chock-full of genius millennials hyped on caffeine and coding. A receptionist took my name and offered me water before she picked up her phone to relay my presence.

"A Mr. Hobbertson is here to see you." Her voice was small and liquid. *Agent Hobbertson*, I corrected her in my mind. I didn't want to start out on the wrong foot. I was already more likely to slip up and say the wrong thing in front of Roman. I suddenly felt scrawny and perhaps too thin. The mental sewage of insecurity was beginning to bubble up.

During my brisk walk to the RF office that morning, I had tried to think of the Phillies current record, the potential SEPTA strike, anything and everything to keep my mind off the omnipresent topic that was devouring all of my errant thoughts. On my walk down Market Street, I focused on each piece of liter that I passed, eyeing the scraps of trash and discarded paper cups. I had actually begun to count them. The effect was very positive. I had a new resolution to volunteer for a city clean-up project and I had successfully kept Avila from my thoughts for a decent duration of time. Sitting in that waiting area though, there was very little to distract myself with. I couldn't stare at the office workers without appearing hostile or odd. I focused instead on my knuckles, but they weren't very interesting.

Finally, the receptionist, with her tightly wound and pinned back strawberry-blonde hair, called me to follow her to Mr. Trecki's office. She was the very picture of northern city women with her gray pencil skirt and black cardigan.

I remained focused on the clean cut of the receptionist's clothes and the calm patterns on the Berber carpet to keep my mind distracted as I followed her. It seemed that with each step the suppressed thoughts were creeping in.

You need to focus. *Think of the case. Keep the details fresh in your mind.* I thought about the specific request I needed to make, the impact it would have on the case, and preventing such egregious abuses and fraud from proliferating. *Yes, proliferating, use that word when Trecki asks for a reason!* I remember thinking that it would be such an excellent verb and that I would look more competent if I used it.

As the receptionist reached the door, I saw her delicate hands tap lightly on the wooden panel. Her light hair appeared darker for a moment and my mind played the cruelest of jokes on me. As she began to turn around, I felt cold sweat on my neck, my heart began to race, and I braced for impact. In that fraction of a second, I was positive she had transformed into Avila. Her hair turning colors before my eyes, her skin draining of color and hue, and her teeth bared in a snarl.

But this was a neurotic trick of my psyche. She was in fact still the receptionist. I must have had the look of death on my face. She patted me on the shoulder and said, "Mr.

Trecki is a nice man. Not like those other types of CEOs that you hear about. You'll do fine."

With her sensitive grace she was gone and I was left with an ajar door in front of me and a mouth as dry as the Sahara Desert.

I stepped into his office. It was small, but it had the illusion of space with a very Spartan design. There was the desk, metal and glass, with some files on top of it and a high-powered laptop hooked up to multiple monitors. There were two wire-framed chairs in front of the desk and wide lanes on either side. The man behind the desk was turned away from me, looking at one of the drawers in the cabinet behind the desk. He was seated and his twisted back gave him the illusion of a hunchback, which I will admit did give me a moment to disarm the man mentally.

The morning sun poured into the room and gave everything a clean look, but there were still dust-mites twirling and dancing in the errant rays of light. I had pictured him sitting in a cramped basement without any windows and heaps of files towering and spilling onto the floor. I should have expected more from the man who built such a powerful company, but you have to keep in mind that first impressions lie heavy on the brain. When I first heard mention of him, at that small party years ago, I pictured a starved and flailing entrepreneur. I wasn't prepared to face his professional success, especially when it compared to his success in the case of our mutual –

"Love," I heard the sandpaper voice say.

"What?" I responded without any thought, my tone cruel and quick. *Had he just read my mind?*

"Hello?" Roman asked again. What I heard was my own version of his parapraxis, what I hoped he would say to start the conversation; the conversation that I wished would never happen. He was now facing me and he was staring at me with his eyebrows raised. His expression posing the question: *Are you okay?*

"Yes, hello," I snapped back into the reality of the moment. "Thank you for taking time to meet with me. I am Special Agent Hobbertson." I extended my arm to shake his hand.

He cautiously leaned forward and reached his hand out. He didn't even get up out of his seat, which I took as a sign of his self-perceived superiority. He was indeed handsome, and looked about the same as he had when I had looked him up on social media years before. He was tan with dark features; his forearms were visible and they were toned. Unconsciously, I covered my right forearm with my left hand.

"Roman Trecki. Glad to be of service when the nation calls. How can I help you?" Roman sat with his arms folded in front of him. He quickly reached across and pressed the small button on his monitor, shutting off the display. He was either trying to hide something, or trying to give me his undivided attention. I still can't be sure which it was.

"Yes, as I explained to your receptionist yesterday …" I went into the long explanation about the Traveler, who I referred to as the suspect for the sake of appearing professional. I explained how he was manipulating the RF servers to hide his fraud. Roman nodded along and listened acutely. He scribbled a quick note on a small pad of paper next to his left hand. He held his pen the way a right-handed person would, but he wrote with his left. He didn't have the curved wrist movement and the dragging motion so prevalent among lefties. I was distracted by this observation as I came to the end of my explanation.

In the brief moment where my monologue lapsed, Roman interjected. "So, you want access to the logs to get the evidence to accurately pin-point this guy and prosecute him." He furrowed his brow and his arms were taught. His hairline was sharp and well defined, but his short haircut revealed the slightest hint of gray pepper through his nondescript brown hair.

"Uh, yes. That is exactly what I would like." I was pleased with his candid ability to grasp the concepts presented.

"Well, you didn't need to meet with me to do that. You could have sent a warrant over to our security team." He looked at me as though he were interrogating me. Had he been equally dreading this meeting? Had he also scanned through my social feeds with trepidation that morning?

"I prefer to work on good faith with people. No one wants their system to be the one known for criminal activity. No one wants to see their company's name dragged through the mud. I find that asking for help is often the easiest option."

Roman smiled and turned his head towards the window. He nodded and prepared to respond. His eyes narrowed in the direct sunlight, but he seemed to be coming to a decision of some kind. "You realize that this puts me in a precarious situation."

I was not expecting that. *Was he referring to Avila? Was he about to delay the work of a federal agency over an ex-girlfriend?*

"How so?" I wanted him to say it. I wanted him to spell it out and put it on the line. *Come on Roman, just admit that you and Avila are out to get me!*

"You know, most of the people that use RF for their website are bloggers, small businesses, and generally good people. I want to cooperate with your investigation, but I also want to be sensitive to the general climate of distrust that surrounds the federal government and its agencies."

Oh, that was a much more logical and valid reason.

"Of course," I responded and nodded my head while I was trying to formulate a response. "We don't want you to appear to be feeding your clients to the wolves, but keep in mind that the websites that are being used in this process likely have no idea that their pages are being manipulated. You are also helping those bloggers and small business owners when you help us."

He held up his hand as though to stop me.

"I want to help you Agent Hobbertson, but I thought about this yesterday. I am within my rights to refuse and request that you produce a warrant. This gives me a way to help you, but to also defer any suspicion that our policy is to just hand out information to the Feds."

I had to cut him some slack, he had thought out the request and anticipated my next moves. I reached into the breast pocket of my blazer and produced the warrant.

"I like to come prepared." I smiled congenially as I handed the document over to him. He read through the warrant and inspected the signature.

He looked up from the document and smirked. His cheeks dimpled and he let out a soft laugh. "Excellent, I will ask Tracey to show you to our system team and they can provide you with the exact information that you need."

"We would actually prefer if the data could be handed over via a portable hard drive. If we go to court, we will need to present the evidence and have it reviewed on multiple occasions. I can't just say, 'well, I saw the logs.'" Roman seemed to have taken that comment as a shock.

"Ah, yeah I guess that does make sense." He folded up the warrant and handed it back to me.

"I brought a clean portable drive with me as well," the thin but dense drive was in my left pants-pocket. It was powerful and compact. It always seemed weird every time I had to mention that I happened to have a 2 terabyte hard-drive in my pants. It never worked well as a joke. I really did have a hard drive in my pocket.

"Well, in this case, I may insist that you use one of our hard-drives. Otherwise, you'll spend forever trying to get past the encryption." He reached around into one of the cabinets behind him. His torso was almost completely twisted around when he managed to palm the drive. He composed himself and handed it to me from across the desk.

"Great, thank you Mr. Trecki." I began to stand up. *That wasn't so bad*, I began to think to myself. But I also began to wonder if, that was it? All of my mental anguish that week and now a passive and easy interaction. Granted, Avila wasn't Roman. I couldn't blame him for her actions. But I had been so focused on her friendship with him that I had come to unilaterally associate him with our break-up.

"Call me Roman," he said kindly. "This meeting was quicker than I thought it would be, I'll save Tracey the trip and introduce you to the team myself."

I watched him as he reversed and wheeled himself around the desk. His unusual actions now made more sense. *He didn't stand to shake my hand because he couldn't.* I started to feel like the real jerk: able-bodied and secretly harboring a hatred of a man who was in a wheelchair. Then I recalled one of the first things Avila ever said to me about him. *'We've shared a common tragedy, that is a bond that isn't easily broken, I don't except you to understand.'"* Perhaps the injury that cost him his mobility was related to that tragedy.

Roman must have caught my eyes as they followed the wheels on his chair. "Eh, you should see the other guy," he uttered in an inconsequential manner.

"Oh really?" I was genuinely shocked by his comment, and somewhat embarrassed to be caught looking so directly at his wheels.

"Yeah, a 30-foot flat sheet of granite." My reaction must have been enough of an invitation to elaborate. "Squirrel suit diving in Brazil earlier this year. The physical therapy is going well. I expect to be out of the chair in a month or so." Roman wheeled himself ahead of me and reversed, backing into the door of this office to push it open.

"Wow, that's pretty extreme." I was genuinely impressed, intrigued, and intimidated in equal parts.

"Yeah, I'm lucky to be alive and all that good stuff. I'm just so sick of this dang chair." Roman led me down the hallway past the reception area and to a small room. He rapped on the door and a few moments later a gawky young man appeared, wide-eyed and skittish.

"Is this a test?" he asked in a matter-of-fact tone.

"No Jake, this isn't a test. I can't see the entire keypad to enter the code. It's okay, you can let me in." I estimated that Roman wasn't exaggerating. The keypad for this door was at eye-level for a standing adult. He might have been able to punch in the keys if he had memorized the code, but he would have risked fat-fingering the numbers.

The young man, who Roman called Jake, looked at his boss through the thin glass in the door and then looked over to me.

"What about him?"

"He's a federal agent," Roman's scratchy voice sounded gruff and firm.

"Oh, well. Okay." The young man opened the door and allowed us both in.

"Thank you," Roman said as he wheeled into the server room. "Jake, I would like you to meet Agent Hobbertson with the FBI."

"Hello." Jake nodded and waited for further information from Roman. He pushed his glasses up on the bridge of his nose. I made a small gesture to begin to extend my hand, but quickly realized that Jake was not the type to shake hands. He was already back at his chair by the time Roman and I were past the door frame. *So, there was a windowless room after all*, I thought as I scanned the layout of the space.

"Jake, Agent Hobbertson has a very specific warrant for information. We value our user's privacy here, but we don't want to be played for suckers if people are using our sites to commit fraud."

"Of course," Jake gave a clipped respose. He pushed his glasses up on his nose again, it was obviously a nervous tick. They were practically flat against the bridge of his nose.

"Let's load the data in this warrant onto one of our

portable drives and then Agent Hobbertson can be on his way." Roman was instructing Jake like a school-teacher. I became mildly suspicious about what information they might be hiding, but my realm was financial crimes. I wasn't going to start digging into other matters, especially given the glaring conflict of interest that I was avoiding.

"Yes, sir," Jake reached out his hand to me, wordlessly requesting the warrant. Within a few moments all of the information I needed was loaded and ready to go.

Jake handed over the external drive, it was still warm from the recent surge of data deposited into the block. Roman thanked Jake and left him to his secure room. The entire situation had been very transactional, as though this employee had actually been a robot, or a manifestation of the computer logs in human form.

Jake appeared relieved to be left alone again. *Some people just work better with machines.* On the way back to reception Roman explained that Jake was the only employee he trusted with the server data and that he took his job very seriously.

As we reached the receptionist's desk, Roman said his farewell before wheeling himself back to his office. "Tracey can assist you with anything else that you need. Hopefully you will be able to close your case now."

"Yes, thank you." I was left standing with the hard-drive. Diligent Tracey was sitting behind her desk, paying attention to the interaction with great detail.

I stood there for a silent moment, trying to make sense of the miss-matched emotions in my head. *He was congenial and polite. But he must know who I am. Perhaps he doesn't care who Avila was with after they broke up. Perhaps he hasn't kept up with her at all. Or maybe, they are still together and they will have a laugh at my expense later this evening.* I couldn't help but think how cruel Avila was.

"Is there anything else I can help you with Mr. Hobbertson?" Tracey asked. She was either ignorant of the proper address being 'Agent' or she was intentionally trying to get under my skin.

I was about to say, "no, I'm good" and walk out when I had a wicked little thought. *I wonder what he is doing on Friday?*

"Yes, actually. We usually can wrap up these technology-related cases pretty quickly. I'd like to be able to stop by and thank Mr. Trecki for his help once we've made our arrest. Is he busy this Friday?"

"He is in meetings all morning and then he is leaving early for an event." Tracey didn't even need to glance at the screen. She had his schedule memorized.

"Oh well. I'll have to make a note to stop by on Monday then." I smiled, but I could sense that Tracey wasn't fooled by my farce. She returned a smile, but I could see that she was being polite by the ways her eyes narrowed and evaluated me.

"Have a nice day Mr. Hobbertson." She emphasized the '*Mister*' with extra care.

"Thank you," I walked away before I could return a verbal barb and make myself look even more like a fool.

The interaction with Roman had been easier than planned. I handed off the hard-drive to our team that specialized in scrubbing data and securing it for evidence. All I had to do was wait for the final confirmation and file the request for the arrest warrant. The Traveler was in my sights.

I filled in Director Knight, but left out the internal mental dialog I had throughout the meeting with Roman Trecki. Knight seemed pleased by my recounting of Roman's concerns over privacy and his insistence on a search warrant.

"What did I tell you? Always have the warrant as a back-up." He gestured with his index finger as though he was pointing to that exact memory on an invisible string in his office.

"You sure did," I nodded and let the man enjoy his moment to recount and retell the same lessons he had already verbalized. Knight was a man of nostalgia, he thrived on retelling the same anecdotes and stories over and over. I could tell that he rehearsed the timing and the pauses. No doubt, this moment would end up becoming a lesson that he would verbally share with new agents. He would likely add on a few embellishments.

I was too anxious to eat as I waited for the final notification from the data team. I paced by the desk and then started to meticulously organize my files. I had a few bad guys to look into, but my focus was zeroed-in on the man who had almost enough money to make a clean get-away. I had closed-in on the Traveler so easily. Maybe the Traveler was trying to become incarcerated so that he could live off of the system permanently. Perhaps he was really looking to make off with a lifetime of free meals, cable TV, and endless free time to read. Stranger things had been recorded in FBI history.

Finally, at 2 pm I heard the muted ping that indicated a new e-mail had come into my Outlook inbox. I checked the results and sure enough, Traveler was working out of a house in Seattle. I met with Knight immediately to coordinate an arrest with the Seattle field office. I filed the papers for an arrest warrant. I made extremely detailed notes that would be sent over to my counterpart on the west coast.

I did finally grab a sandwich as I waited for a response from the team in Seattle. We held a conference call at the end of the day and had everything coordinated for a quick arrest. Both Knight and I stressed the urgency of the matter and the potential flight-risk of the suspect given the amount of money that he pilfered.

Knight concluded the call and asked that we be kept up-to-date on the operation. The plan was for an early morning raid the following day. Early morning for the Seattle team meant normal time for us on the east coast. We had a plan in place. I told Knight I would be in much earlier than usual to be able to handle any last-minute issues, should they come up.

It was well past 8 pm when I left the office. I was excited to know that we were so close to catching the Traveler, but I felt the usual wave of worry knowing that there would be a few more hours where this man was free to steal again, and free to run.

I made my way home along the dark streets of my city. I found a calm in the sounds of my footsteps along the pavement, just mine alone. I took a longer route home and passed by Independence Mall, empty except for a few errant tourists snapping photos. The bell tower was lit impeccably and the visitor center was quiet. As the others left the park, I could have fooled myself for a moment that I wasn't in a modern century. In the darkness, Philadelphia always looks so revolutionary.

The evening was cool. Fall was well on its way and there was no amount of wishing or longing for summer that could stop it. I found my mind wandering to the long walks I had taken through the city. Usually I was going somewhere, always aiming for a specific destination. That night I recalled the most aimless of my walks, the one that served as my purgatory and my punishment.

I still can't even remember exactly how that argument began, all those years ago. It must have been like the others. In my memory, I had reviewed it so many times and tried to make sense of the order of who threw what words at each other and when, that I must have rearranged them at some point. I knew that I had been growing more and more jealous of the time Avila was spending without me. I was suspicious of her time with friends, *was she really with friends or was she with Roman?* She called me out on my attempts to control who she was seeing and what she was doing with her time. I accused her of cheating. She accused me of being paranoid.

In that moment I was so overwhelmed with contempt, I felt that Avila's words had started to attack me.

So, I lost control.

I snapped and I hit her square in the jaw. Not with an open-palmed slap, but with a clenched fist. Avila absorbed the full force of it and stared at me, shocked and scared. Her skin instantly flashed red and her eyes began to well with tears. Pain consumed her expression.

I left right then, without a word. I wandered the city aimlessly throughout that night. Once dawn broke, I found a diner. I stayed until that afternoon when I found a bar. I didn't return to the scene of that last interaction, the scene of my crime, until it was evening again. As I expected, and hoped, she was gone.

That's right, I just left. I'm the bad guy all along.

At least I was. I'm not a bad guy now and I would never- I guess it doesn't matter what I say now. I'm condemned, by myself, by her, by you. Worst of all, her punishment will be slow, drawn out, and incredibly detailed.

That's it. That is the root of the fear that was consuming me. I was waiting for her worst, her detailed and piercing cross-examination of my personality, my flaws, and my motives for being the guy that hit her.

That is the reason why I was the perfect specimen for a revenge novel, I am the villain in her story. After all, the novel was titled *Scarlett: Avenged.* It had to be my turn, it just had to be.

The walk down memory lane did nothing but enflame my already anxious mind. When I reached my apartment, I sat pensively on my couch, hunched over and finally being honest with myself.

I knew that soon, once the book was released, the written character that was supposed to represent me would be hated by many. They will shake their heads as they read the details of my appearance, my walk, my swagger. The words would bleed before my eyes and stain my hands like red stamp ink as I read the passage that detailed what I did that evening: the violence and the cowardice.

I never spoke to her again after that night. I knew that anything I could say would just sound cliché and would feel false on my tongue. I stayed silent. Might she have noticed that it was a penitent silence? Would Avila forgive my moment of rage and recognize the many good moments that we had before that horrible night?

I had stopped drinking for a time after our relationship ended. I was convinced that my fit of rage must have been sourced from a well of fire in my stomach. I stopped going out to the bars where the music was loud and the lights were low. I could feel her presence there, following me, reverberating from the deep bass line. I spent a long time denying myself any entertainment or fun, until, little by little, I broke back into my normal routines.

The words from the *Philadelphia Magazine* interview rang fresh in my mind, emblazoned and empowered.

> *"Scarlett may be investigating paranormal activities, but it is always human errors that bring her back into this world.* ***I wanted to focus on an issue that is important not just to women, but to society. We can't just say this is a woman's issue anymore, it's a human issue.*** *Through Scarlett I can bring this problem to the forefront of our consciousness and hopefully spur change."*

There could be no mistaking her words. My time was up. Avila was ready to disclose her true hatred for me and avenge herself through Scarlett.

I closed my eyes that night as I tried to fall asleep. All that I could see where those piercing green eyes from the poster. They were staring at me. Like Fitzgerald's oculist, her eyes could see all, silently passing judgment.

After another night of little to no sleep, Thursday morning came unwanted and unwelcomed. I set an alarm to get up earlier than usual and each inch of my body resisted the blaring sound, urging me to get up, to move, and to get to work.

I purchased two large coffees on the way into the office and found that Director Knight was in his office, scanning through some documents. He thanked me for the coffee and we both headed to our conference room to wait for verbal and visual confirmation of the raid and arrest. This would be yet another small success on my pile of "always trying to prove to myself that I am a successful person."

As I continue to tell you the events of that week, the pre-amble to a significant turning point in my life, know that even further back into my past was a tumultuous and rolling relationship with Avila. We had glorious moments of happiness and affection. But within her was an independence. Something forcefully uncontrollable that couldn't be restrained. She saw no issue on the topic of staying in contact with her ex, Roman, and no ability to see the mistrust from my point of view. Within me, contempt started to brew, bubble, and ferment. I couldn't get her to see my side and now everyone in the world would only know her side. It felt so unfair, I felt so jilted by my impending punishment. But, with each successful case closed, I began to feel more self-affirmed. I began to feel the confidence that had once defined me, begin to breathe life back into me. That morning was about so much more than another arrest; it was about proving that I was still right.

I was unfocused and exhausted that morning. I should have been alert. I should have been thinking through all of the possible methods for the raid to go wrong. But I was distracted by the looming deadline for Scarlett: Avenged to be released.

I brought my laptop into the conference room to check

through emails as the video feed was set up. I clicked through some smaller items that didn't require my attention and then sorted them away. I saw a few red flags pop-up for new fraud activity. It appeared as though several new bad guys were popping up and all using the same method of hacking into gift cards, but they were all using new websites that I hadn't encountered before. After a quick glance, I could see that none of them ran through the RF server.

My cognitive gears were firing on a delay; however, my synapses were finally starting to wake up. I checked the usual routes of the Traveler. It appeared that he had tried to make another large deposit in the late evening hours, but was blocked. I began to come to the realization; *RF would have closed the potential loophole as soon as I left so as to keep this kind of activity from persisting.*

That would have tipped off the Traveler for sure. The new flags that I registered in the early hours of that Thursday morning could have been new activity, or it could have been this same exact guy trying to finish off his scheme before leaving.

Director Knight was sipping on his coffee and eyeing the video screen, peering above the rim of his glasses. The agents were starting to take their places flanking each other outside of the apartment. "We should check to see if this guy has made any travel plans." I was trying to hide the panic in my voice.

"What?" Director Knight muttered; his attention fully focused on the video screen.

"I think he may have already left; we should call these agents back." I tried to keep my voice level to mask how problematic the situation was.

"Huh?" Knight finally looked over at me, just as the agents on the video screen were using a battering-ram to break down the suspect's apartment door.

"I think he split early. He won't be there." I turned my attention to the screen. The chaos of watching a half-dozen agents burst into an apartment from the viewpoint of a thin camera was jarring. The constantly moving picture left me nauseated as we waited for some kind of signal that the suspect was captured. What we heard instead was that the apartment was empty.

"No one here," a voice managed to squeeze through the radio static. "Place is empty, must have been tipped off."

Indeed, the Traveler had been tipped off and was on his way. When his usual path had been blocked through Roman's Forum he found an alternative route, transferred the money quickly, and took off. While this was in the criminal's nature to evade us, I was supposed to keep us one step ahead.

As the agents began to set about the work of cataloging the items remaining in the apartment, a loud pop came through the thin speakers in the conference room and the video screen went blank. After frantic calls we confirmed that a small explosive device did go off in the apartment. While it wasn't big enough to cause structural damage, several agents were burned. Those moments, those hours, passed around me like water. They felt like a numbing cold stream crossing over me, burying me, drowning me beneath its weight.

All of my small successes paled in comparison to this glaring error in judgment. It was the item I had neglected, and my preoccupation with Avila was to blame. Director Knight had signed off of the conference call, I was too shamed to speak. For a mild-mannered man, he sure could berate an employee.

If my head was hanging low that morning after the muffed arrest and explosion, it continued to droop and sag throughout the day. I had to file paperwork, answer to Director Knight's boss, hear the chatter in the breakroom stop abruptly as I walked in, and try to track the Traveler through airline and bus records. I confirmed that the injured agents were released from the hospital and that they would return to desk-duty quickly. My only small grace was that they were not more severely injured.

The one shining ray of hope in that week of torture, my career, was considerably dimmer that afternoon.

I was in need of solace, but I had been single for months. I regretted intentionally misplacing the phone number of my Sunday evening rendezvous, wishing for some kind of human interaction to distract me. I stood outside of the office, bracing my neck against the chilly wind by folding up the collar on my jacket. After thumbing through my phone, I realized that I had never responded to Nick's texts earlier in the week. I opened up the conversation and typed a short response:

"Yeah, I'm alright. You? Drinks?"

I wasn't about to pour out my frustrations in a text message and I was loath to express them verbally as well. I wondered if the catharsis of drinking with an old friend would coax my emotions from their caged den within my mind. Perhaps if I released all of those demons, I would exorcise of them for good.

I began walking aimlessly up Market Street. Every few blocks I would look back at City Hall, illuminated and omnipresent. I didn't go a day without passing it and I never tired of it. I stood admiring the structure and felt my phone buzz in my pocket.

"Yeah man. About to catch a train home, but I can stay for another hour to catch up."

Nick usually took the train through 30th Street Station each morning and evening on his way out to the suburbs. He and Claudette had moved out to Upper Dublin at some point in the previous year and now he was a regular commuter. I made a note to give him grief for living in what had so lovingly been nicknamed "Upper Dumpster."

"Not far from 30th Street myself. Sláinte?"

I started to make my way further up Market Street without waiting for Nick's response. I felt my phone buzz with his response "Here" as I crossed the street to enter the bar.

It was unfortunately a packed house. University professors and young professionals gathered for a weekly round of some quiz game that had become somewhat boisterous. Nick and I took our seats at the far end of the bar. I thought of ordering a gluten-free beer, but decided to dive in fully and drown my tormented sorrows in whiskey and Coke.

"Hitting the hard stuff early man?" Nick inquired after I placed my order, definitely a harder drink compared to the orange-and-lime beer that he had ordered.

"Us unmarried guys get to do that every once in a while," I gave him a sly smile that invited him to tell me about his life with Claudette. They were happy with their new house. He was doing some projects to get the house into better shape, which helped to build on his limited skills.

In short order, the conversation turned to focus on what was new in my life. Usually, I would answer these kinds of questions with vague updates about how much I loved me job. I didn't have much going on in my life outside of work; I had been so solitary and standoffish that my personal life was like a sinkhole, ever-empty and dangerous to approach. Since I had a bad day at work, I didn't necessarily want to boast about how well I was doing. I knew that one botched mission was unlikely to result in my dismissal, but I was fairly glum about my prospects that evening.

"Not much actually, not much at all," I took a hard and open swallow of my drink.

"Yeah," Nick offered sympathetically. It wasn't as though he was aware of how bleak my social outlook was, but he had to know that it wasn't good. "I'm sure this week doesn't make it any easier for you."

I wanted to defend myself and spurn his insights, but hadn't this been the reason that I had reached out to him? "Ah, yep. It's been tougher this time around." I nodded in agreement but couldn't make eye contact with him.

"Well, especially after we all thought that she was done writing for good." I could see him shrug in my peripheral vision. I wanted to nod along, but this was news to me. *She can't give up writing, it's her passion*, I thought instinctively. Even though her retirement would have saved me from that week of hell, it would have meant that the cat-and-mouse game that she was playing with my mind would officially be over.

And then I realized, as the whiskey began to soak into my stomach and loosen up my thoughts, that I hadn't thought much about what Avila was doing. I was focused on what I had done. I was fixated on that moment when I saw the betrayal in her eyes and had been bracing for retribution. I had spent all of that time focused on single-state Avila. The Avila who was scorned and angry, the monster of my dreams. But I hadn't taken much time to think of the giddy and excited Avila who just found out her book would become a movie, or the consciously humble Avila who was making great efforts to be gracious, or the exhausted Avila who struggled with the pressures of quick success. I had discarded all of those other versions and ignored any other possible emotion to maintain my villainous version of the person that she was.

"Uh, was she done?" I asked quietly, hoping my words would be small enough to be missed and the truth avoided.

"Yeah, yeah. She lived abroad for a year and didn't write a single word except for a few postcards home. Claudette was worried that she would have to fly over to whatever small little village she was in and shake her out of her funk, but it seems that time away actually brought her to this - " Nick paused, searching and scanning his memory for an exact word as though it were a tactile object he could pick out from the menu of beers hanging above the bar. "- Higher plane of her career." He finished his thought and took the last swig of his beer.

"Oh, wow," my voice did not echo the enthusiasm of my word choice.

"I know you probably don't want to talk about it much. It's okay. I'm here if you ever want to catch up man, but I think I need to run if I'm going to catch my train." Here was the opportunity to openly discuss the one topic that was voraciously eating into my grey-matter and Nick was leaving.

"Yeah, of course," I offered without much thought, filling the sound space with my words. "Will you be at the uh, thing tomorrow night?"

"No," he shook his head and waved his hand to display how emphatically he didn't want to go. "It's gonna be a little stuffy and we'll see Avila when she is around this weekend." His delicate manner of side-stepping her name and circumventing her had been replaced by the casual indifference of a person whose mind was focused elsewhere. He was thinking about catching his train, I was focused on catching the woman who was about to ruin my life.

"Do you know for sure if I have a reason to worry tomorrow?" I looked at my shoes. My raw and unhidden, unabashed misery was apparent in the sag of my shoulders, the stoop of my neck, and the trembling of my hands that were shoved into my pockets.

"Hey man," he beckoned me to look up. "You gotta stop worrying about this. If she did, she did. If she didn't, she didn't. I really think you aren't giving her enough credit." I could see his patience had sublimated and was now being sucked into the air vents and whisked away on the wind. He looked at me with pity.

It had been to Claudette's that Avila had fled that evening, with a loose story about tripping clumsily as she was trying to pack her things and leave. The bruise would have been obvious though. Claudette hated me from that moment on. Nick had given me the benefit of his doubt, but my behavior and worry must have exposed me by now. The look in Nick's eyes was shouting, *she could have sued you, she could have had you arrested, so maybe be quiet and take this like a man.* All of those things would have been true; perhaps I should have been more grateful for the career that I had been able to keep. But I despised the idea of being indebted to her, to that act. I didn't want to be captive for committing one crime for the rest of my life.

When I think back on that lonely evening of drinks with Nick, I realize how captive I was to my victimhood. I was so indignant in my right to be the one who was belittled and abused in that scenario. *What right did she have to use her experience in our relationship, of which I owned a 50% stake, in her creative works?* In the months that followed those fateful twenty-four hours, I have realized that I had no right to feel any ownership over her thoughts and feelings. If only I would have realized that years earlier, I might have saved myself heartache and Avila a black eye.

This hindsight is so startlingly clear, but that evening was so dark that I can only remember the stark shining street lights, the brown glow of the buildings and sidewalks, and the pitch-black sky reflected on a city full of glass windows. At first, I walked quickly, my steps echoing the anger inside of me. With each firm clap of my feet on the cement I felt the satisfaction of the sound until I found myself intentionally stomping with each step to create a louder and louder sound. I would not be quiet; I would be cantankerous and impossible to avoid.

Without really trying to, I walked by *the* book store. Closed and dark, the street reflected clearly on the slick glass of the storefront. I could see a stark reflection of my outline, with the empty park and the nearby lights. Behind the glass, separating me from the instrument of my insanity were the posters of Avila's staring eyes and an artfully stacked pile of her book, *Scarlett: Avenged.* A hundred pairs of her eyes glared at me, like a giant arachnid with its prey ensnared. I was looking back into my doom.

I pondered my predicament for a while on that street. No one else was around, which was eerie and peculiar. I began to think of what last desperate acts I could make to stop the next day from coming. I could find a brick, a stray rock, or a heavy trashcan and throw it into the glass. I would shatter that clean and smooth poster and send the books tumbling. I could criminally maneuver a way into the back of the store and steal the volumes of the freshly printed novel and squirrel them away so that no one could ever read the words in my hoard. I could pile each of those books in the center of the store and strike a match to watch her words burn.

I went so far as to think of pulling a different book from the shelves. Perhaps one that had an inflammatory message, so as to avoid suspicion. If a crazed religious nut broke into the bookstore and burned every version of the latest romance novel or some magic-based series for children, and Avila's book just happened to be burned up in the process, I would distance myself from suspicion. I envisioned the investigation that would follow and that the inspector would not be focused on those with a known aversion to Avila.

The plans unfolded in my head so easily, I could easily explain my alibi and make it home quickly to get a verified location at the time of the crime. I knew the master code to disarm several alarm systems. I figured that there would be a janitor's closet or a storage room with some kind of combustible chemicals to spray over the books. I was skint on matches, but made a mental note to check for some in the drawers behind the cash register.

I would have gone through with it all too, if it hadn't become abundantly obvious that I wouldn't be able to destroy every copy in the city, let alone every copy in the state or country. The book would likely be available online as well; it would find its way into millions of homes on illuminated screens. I wanted to rip out the pages that would reference the fictionalized character that Avila had written to represent me. I wanted to read it now and brace for the impact. I was so certain that she would have used this opportunity to rat me out and write me in. My hands clenched into fists reflexively as my mind spun around this new idea. I began to look around me for something to throw at the window.

To my left and right the sidewalk was clear except for imperceptible pebbles trapped in the cracks between the sidewalk blocks. No large chunk of cement broken off, no slate rock to throw. No stray bricks from the road were popping up. The closest trash can appeared to be bolted to the ground, so I knew that would be a non-starter.

The lack of resources exasperated me and validated that this evil plan should not be carried out. I stuck my fists into my jacket pocket and turned to walk home. It was a day of ruined plans.

I turned the corner and kept my head down against the wind blowing between the buildings. I passed the alley that was lined with dumpsters, where the back door to the bookstore would have been. I passed the additional posters advertising the event and continued past other closed store fronts. I was almost to the end of the block, with a clear right-of-way to continue walking, when I almost tripped on it.

I was so eager to cross the street in time to make the light, that I missed the rounded and bulbous rock. It was sitting precariously in the middle of the sidewalk and appeared to have been carefully placed there. How could it have made its way onto that exact street and into that position otherwise?

I could have picked it up, ran back to the store, and hurled the object in a matter of seconds. It appeared to me as a gift from the universe, a chance to stop the clock on my deadline with perpetual embarrassment and shame. I pictured my arm arching back and chucking the rock. I could almost hear the last shards of glass tinkling as they rained down on each other. My arm muscles began to twitch, as though anticipating the force about to be exerted. But I couldn't move. I was frozen between indecision and uncharacteristic action. Would my arm throw another blow to Avila, this time bruising and scaring her professional face? Would I find the strength to just walk away and move on?

After another moment, I heard footsteps behind me, another late-night pedestrian out on the streets. I realized that my firm stance on the sidewalk would appear unusual at best. I began walking, being forced to move along before deciding. Fate interceded to save me from criminal activity that evening. I found my way home and poured myself another glass of whiskey before slipping into an amber colored sleep.

I spent that night in a vivid dream. The streets of my city, my beloved Philadelphia, were laid out like the pages of a book. As I crossed each intersection, the pages would flip, revealing new text. But as these thoughts became words, they turned out to be one word in repetition: "Avila." The pages were covered in a steady stream of her name over and over again. "Avila Avila Avila Avila Avila Avila Avila Avila," the words ran across in printed type. They were the ticker-tape of my thoughts from that past week. More accurately, they were my thoughts over the past years. I was obsessed, it was plain as day when it was all written out. Paper clouds formed above my head and began to let out the smallest little raindrops comprised of scraps of paper. In the paper-motion film-like dream, I continued to walk until finally I reached out my hand and grabbed one of the raindrops. I unfolded it and written within was, of course, "Avila." This mania was ever so transparent now.

This dream lingered with me even as I settled into my

desk at work and scanned for the latest flags. The search was taking longer to run that morning so I got my coffee and avoided making eye contact with Director Knight as we crossed paths in the hallway. He didn't make an attempt to say hello. Perhaps he was avoiding me as well.

When I returned to my desk and unlocked my screen it appeared as though an outbreak of measles or smallpox had invaded my system. Bright red flags littered my results screen, hundreds of entries deep instead of the usual dozen or so that were usually marked each morning. I checked my filters thinking that I must have made an error in the search parameters. But this was in fact the activity over the course of one day. It appeared to be an over-night explosion in gift-card fraud. I followed through on the flags and found that overnight there had been a dozen new sites started on the RF server that were created for the sole purpose of laundering the stolen gift card values.

It would appear that until additional measures were put into place, I would have to be in continual contact with Roman to request log files and that these sites be shut down. I made a note of the new sites that were started and made a point to log the new sites as they appeared to look for any larger patterns that would aid in catching the persons responsible. A chilling thought caught me, *what if it was only one person responsible? What if one person was developing these sites so that other thieves could steal their funds $500 at a time?*

As I sorted through the data, the hours of the day ticked by. I was thankful for the close of business and that I had spent the day avoiding the looming event that would be held only a few blocks from my apartment, and would intersect my route home. I can admit that Avila filled my thoughts in the empty moments of that day. *Was she somewhere hidden among the code, the binary 0s and 1s of the newly discovered treasure trove of fraud? Was this her true torture?*

On my way out of the office that day I stopped to discuss the new data with Director Knight. He mulled over the information as he nodded his head. I expressed my concern over the sudden spike in activity and told him I would leave it alone over the weekend to see what patterns emerged. I planned to pay Roman Trecki and his team a visit on Monday morning if there needed to be additional measures put in place to stop the proliferation of the dummy sites.

Director Knight seemed pleased with my assessment and made a side comment about going too hard on me the day before. I told him that I had made an error and expected no less than to be called out on it. He offered to take me out for a drink, but I demurred, stating that I had plans. It tasted like a prevarication on my tongue and sodium saturated taste-buds. I didn't have plans to meet anyone or to do anything particularly. But I knew that I needed to keep my evening clear. I didn't want to mark the passing of that night with just a happenstance happy hour and a quiet evening of watching the news and reading before bed. I needed to feed my anxiety and confront my demon face-to-face: blazing green eyes and all.

They'll make a netting to ensnare you, to trap you, to catch you in the act. My medusa strands will turn you to stone as they cover and suffocate you.

-Scarlett Moore and the Golden Pegasus

I pondered my predicament on my stroll towards the bookstore. The evening was still young so I popped into a nearby restaurant for a bite to eat. Would Avila be dining there with her friends and manager before the event? *Would Roman be taking her out for a romantic dinner to celebrate the release?* I was dying to be the one to ruin her perfect evening.

The words that Nick had sent to me were streaming constantly through my mind. What perfectly curled and formed letters would be awaiting me if I ever chose to open that book? *Would a gnarled hand reach out to suffocate me? Would those words brush me off in a cavalier manner?* My thoughts were wild. And finally, just as my food arrived, steaming and greasy, I went to the dark place in my own head.

Am I really as bad as Ike Turner or Ray Rice or any of the men who share my crime?

Yes. I know the answer; the answer was and still is "Yes." I may hope for mercy, but I still know the answer. No reasoning or pages of explanation can excuse me and now I live as a man who shouldn't deserve trust. Even though I know I shouldn't have done it and have sworn to never do it again, I still don't find myself deserving of trust.

Perhaps, I wondered, *if Avila writes me out as the monster that I was that evening, I can start to forgive myself.* I had spent a momentous amount of effort fighting myself, hoping that she wouldn't expose my sins in printed word, but I was also hoping for the release. I wanted permission to own up to my evil nature and face her honest appraisals.

Would my crucible of redemption burn at the speed of light? The speed of sound? The speed of literature?

The grease sopped into the bun of my cheeseburger and left if wilting in my hand, the slimy lettuce sliding out as my hands clamped down. My appetite had fled at the thoughts of my internal self-loathing, but I didn't dare to enter the bookstore. Not yet. I didn't want to be one of the first people there, obviously loitering and anxious to catch a glimpse of her.

As I cleared my plate and drowned my fries in ketchup, I began to envision the moment when she might see me. Would it be a smile, glad to see me after so many years? Would she duck her eyes quickly, recognizing me instantly and hoping to avoid an interaction? Would she pass over me quickly, only to realize in a nightmare that evening that I had been so close to her yet again? Or, would she grimace, delighted to see that I had shown up to face my executioner? So much would be revealed in that first interaction. I felt myself anticipating that look, much like I did when I had prepared for our initial dates. I had been anxious to impress her and read her expression.

I paid for my meal and tipped the waitress an extra smile. My hands were trembling so I shoved them into my pockets, but it did nothing to stop the jittering. If anything, the motion was exacerbated by the friction of the cloth, so I withdrew my hands and crossed them behind my back. The sun had set behind the tall buildings and marbled facades. The lights that lined the perimeter of the park, steeped in history and wonder for many a Philadelphian, were lit. I sauntered over and leaned on one of the light-poles, trying to channel the practiced cool of a Humphrey Bogart. It was a failed effort.

I let the moment hang before me. It was so weighty that I could almost see it press down on the leaves of the trees and cause the traffic signs to bend. In my veins I could feel each blood cell as it whizzed by on its way to oxygenate my limbs; I could feel the enzymes as they bounced against the plasma, I could feel each element as it was held in suspended wonder against the force of Bohr's nucleus. I could feel that it was all about to end, my torture would soon be over. I would wake up the next morning as a man free from Avila's grasp.

Finally, when I felt my hands settle and I mustered the courage, I crossed the street to enter the bookshop. The front of the store was already packed with fans eager to get their hands on a copy of Scarlett: Avenged. They were of the mindset that if they had the book before anyone else that they would be counted among the true and worthy fans of Scarlett Moore. I squeezed my way past the hoards and found an empty alleyway formed by two bookshelves. They appeared to have been pushed closer together for the event, so as to make room in the main area of the bookstore. But they were still far enough apart for me to slip through, like a secret channel leading to Avila.

As I breached the opening between the two bookshelves, I saw another large group. This one was sitting quietly, and listening to a tall woman with features so simultaneously dark against skin so pale I couldn't place her nationality. She was wearing a long flowing skirt with a patterned design and a black sweater. Her thick black hair reminded me of a movie star, it appeared to be glamorous and somewhat out of place on a woman who was dressed in a new-age manner. As she spoke, she pointed to a photo of small children. These children were clearly identifiable as slum-children. Their clothes were tattered and either too big or too small. Their smiles were eager and hopeful. It was the kind of image I had seen before, but had passed mindlessly. The woman continued to tell a personal story of the child on the right, a young girl who was doomed to a life in a brothel. This woman, unknown to me, was so captivating that I almost forgot why I was there. I became so entranced in what she was saying that I couldn't blink, I didn't dare move, until I saw *her.*

Sitting in the front row of this grouping of people, I saw the bright glitter of her vibrant hair.

It was almost like a dream coming to life. I could see the ghost of her as I passed by the bookshelves, her apparition always just around the corner. I longed to catch up, but I knew a set of fangs would greet me if I did.

After the woman's speech ended, a man stood up to applaud her and thank her for the information provided. I knew who this man was, though I had never met him in person before. It was Avila's literary agent. He was tall and thin, his graying hair only visible in a small tuft on the crown of his head. He was clearly uncomfortable with the new norms in men's fashion as he was sporting a mismatched outfit that screamed, *'I'm trying to be aloof and I hope you've noticed!"*

He informed the crowd that they would break for a few moments and then Avila would be speaking on the book and reading an excerpt to the crowd. At this she rose and waved to the crowd. Her eyes were kept at the level of those in their seats, she didn't even glance past the bookshelves in the back of the store where I was still lurking. Surely, I thought, if she had spotted me, she would have given some sign. Even if she anticipated my arrival, she wouldn't be able to hide a twitch or a micro-expression on her face.

She may not have noticed me, but I was making a quick study of her. She was much more polished than I remembered. As a younger woman she was more loose and awkward, never so tall and self-assured. Her shoulders were arched back where there used to be a timid slouch. Her clothes were well tailored and suited her body, nothing like the jeans and lumpy sweatshirts that she used to hide herself in. And her hair. Her bright red hair was more vibrant that I had ever pictured in my nightmares. It was so red that it was almost orange. As she subtly moved her head, smiling at another section of the crowd, it moved. Each minute movement looked like flashes of fire dancing around her, like a halo of destruction. She made these subtle movements so quickly and was now excusing herself, moving out of the area to avoid being waylaid by a fan or a reporter.

I moved my eyes around quickly to see if anyone would follow her. Not the reporter that was sitting in the second row, identifiable from his profile picture in the Philadelphia Magazine article. Short and wavy dirty blond hair, ruddy cheeks, and thin silver glasses were enough to be able to tell it was him. The steno pad in hand also helped. The agent had made his way over to the reporter, likely discussing some details.

I also spotted Roman, still in his wheelchair, but clearly

very well dressed. He was trying to catch the attention of the woman that had been speaking. He seemed eager and nervous. Perhaps has was vying for a chance to re-enter Avila's life. *Not so close anymore, are you?* I wondered.

This was my chance. I wanted to act quickly, but I moved slowly, carefully. I was like a crouching cat of prey, moving with the balls of my feet first. I headed around the perimeter of the open seating area and noticed that she had slipped down a hallway. There were three doors: "Men", "Ladies", "Storage." I didn't see her in the hall and didn't want her agent or anyone to see me just standing around waiting for her. In my hasty planning, I just acted and opened up the door marked storage and waited inside. I could easily back away if someone else came by, and they would shut the door, and not notice me lurking. But, if Avila came by, I could still see and take my chance to talk to her. It seemed like a half decent idea in the fraction of a second it took me to think of it.

I should have expected her to be startled. I hadn't really thought through how it must look to her. At first a voice calling to her from the shadows, then me, her ex, stepping out, surprising her. Did I scare her? Did I make her mentally check the exits and calculate whether she should scream or run? Did I have any effect on her at all?

"Oh, hi," Avila said as her eyes widened and her breaths became more shallow. I had forgotten how soft her voice was, how silent she could be when she wasn't projecting to a crowd. For some reason that tiny voice hadn't remained in my memory.

"Hi," was all that I could muster. I had pictured in my mind so many times what I would say to her if we ever came face to face again. But all I could get out was the basic, "Hi."

"Oh, Trevor! Hi!" she pretended to recognize me, I figured this for a ruse. *How could she not recognize me? What a faker,* I knew she must have been faking. "How are you?"

"Uh, okay I guess," the contempt in my voice was uncontrollable. I couldn't hide how annoyed I was at her mental exercises, tricking me and tormenting me. It flooded me all at once and with the tidal wave it caused, it washed away any sentimental outcroppings that might have been budding within me.

Avila, with her long pale legs and tan heels, her overall muted and demure color scheme, didn't fool me. She looked as though she was searching for what to say next, she looked uncomfortable and ready-to-run at the first chance.

"Um, are you here to see Roman again?" she nodded her head towards the party to indicate that Roman was there. *So, he did tell you about our meeting.* This immediately renewed my suspicions that they were in fact back together as a couple.

"No," I shook my head as I jutted my jaw forward. "But I think that we need to talk." I gestured for her to follow me into the store room. After a moment's hesitation she followed. Oh memory, please remind me of how that bright and illuminated hallway could have been the final and anti-climactic chapter in my saga with Avila. But no, it was that dank and dark store room where our story finally came to an end, our journey completed.

Once we were both inside of the store room, I grasped for the light switch, finally taking a wide swing and finding the delicate chain. I gave it a yank and the dark space was sparkly illuminated by a bald bulb swinging from the ceiling. There were stacks of boxes as far as I could see, built into shapes that gave the room depth and texture.

"So, what's up?" Avila asked. There was a tone in her voice that hinted at, *"I need to get back out there, make it quick."* I turned to face her. The illuminated space was small, I could either stand in the shadows to speak to her, or she could stand in the shadows, or we could both stand very close to one another in the light. We naturally struck a middle-distance, both barely visible to one another on the periphery of the illumination.

"I've spent a lot of time this week thinking about you, and the book," I let my words trail off. I was starting to sound like a deranged fan. Why hadn't I thought more about what to say? "And, I thought about your old habits of writing your exes into your novels."

I heard her let out a deep sigh. She didn't start to reply, which emboldened my suspicions. Instead, she made it clear that her exhausted release of air was not an admission of guilt, but of a pained and repeated defense that she had made so many times.

"I considered writing a book with you as a main character. I started the manuscript. But it was rubbish, it wasn't my style or my genre. It felt all wrong."

"What genre, romance?" I made a point to put that little wolfish smile on my face, the one she used to always say made her melt. It was my secret weapon to wiggle back into her heart.

"No, true-crime." She responded plainly, unblinking with her cavalier answer.

"Well, I know what you've been up to. Haven't you made me suffer enough?"

"Suffer? What are you talking about?" Her arms were now crossed, her guard was up, and the battle had begun.

"You, waiting and waiting to write me into one of your novels so that you can tell the world how horrible I am!"

"Do you hear yourself, Trevor? Do you?" She pleaded for me to see reason.

"Just own up to it! You've been taunting me and playing with my head ever since. I'm sick of it, just stop!" It felt like all of my worries and fears had been piling up into a tin bucket and they had all just come cascading out. I knew that my voice had been too loud and my final exclamation too shrill.

"Trevor, not everything is about you! I'm not playing any game with you, it's all in your head! It's with yourself!" She made a motion with her hand, as though it could physically shield her from my words, my truth.

"Oh, yeah right! Just admit that you want some revenge on me for what I did. For what happened that night." There it was. In all of the time that we were together and all of the time that we had been apart, that infinitesimal moment of time when my fist connected with her jaw was what defined us. It defined me. It was defining that moment in the store room. It was the center of the dilapidated universe that we had once built with bright planets, celestial orbs, and stars that was now off kilter and filled with the dark void of a singularity.

"What do you want me to say? Huh? You hitting me was the worst thing that could ever happen to me, it damaged me so profoundly that I'll always have you on my mind, and an axe to grind with you? No! I'm not just my past relationships, Trevor. I'm a person with a life and passions that extend beyond my own self. Are you really that short-sighted to not see that?"

Maybe she was right. Maybe I had been inventing this evil version of her in my head for so long to justify what I had done, to assuage my own guilt. Maybe I needed the game to play so that I could blame her instead of myself. I didn't have a response. My silence seemed to embolden her and bring on a new lashing of words. She didn't need to publish a character based on me and make subtle jabs or observances to cut me. She had a direct line to say exactly what she needed to without having to fuddle with subtext and plot.

"OK, Trevor." I had struck a nerve here. "I wanted to hurt you the way that you hurt me. But I realized that would give you the power. That would glamorize what you did." I could tell that she was building up to a larger comment, one that would likely rip me apart. "You're so tormented about how I might tell people about what you did? Why don't you just try apologizing, huh?" She paused as if she thought I might just blurt it out, then and there. "Say it out loud, own up to it. You say you're so sick of being haunted by this, but it's not me that you're mad at. It's yourself."

In that moment I knew that I could react in one of three ways: 1. Forgiveness, the most peace-giving of all outcomes, but might have led to some tears as I struggled with the torrent of emotions welling up in me and start to erase the villainous version of Avila that I had built in my mind. 2. Abject denial and more accusation throwing followed by a brief storming out which would leave me in a dark storeroom playing the role of the crazy ex. What if as she left in a huff, she slipped and hit her head on the slick cement of the store-room? Surely, no one would believe my innocence if she were to crack her skull and go into a coma, or die. Or 3. That I could lose control before I decided between the first two options and attack her. I didn't find any option appealing.

But Avila made the decision for me. She shook her head slowly, pitying me with her eyes and pursed lips. She left silently, just like she did many nights before. I stood in that empty room for some time, not wanting to rush after her. I debated staying in that room until closing, when I could be sure that everyone had left and that no one would see the shame, written so delicately and precisely across my face. In the few moments that passed, I decided to just make a run for it, I would try to slip out through that same narrow opening between the two bookcases.

I headed out into the hallway and could hear Avila's voice coming from the main area. I tried to find my way through the back of the crowd, but the main area was now even more cramped with all of the fans from the front of the store now loitering, shifting their weight as they stood to hear her speak. She was into a story about how her friend, the woman who had been speaking earlier, had told her about the increasing incidences of young girls being kidnapped and sold into the sex trade. Avila remarked that she thought it would make a good mystery, was it a supernatural monster snatching up these girls? Indeed, in was an ancient evil: greed.

I slowly and quietly moved through the crowd, finally catching the words at the bottom of the posters that I had been avoiding with the logo for the non-profit associated with the cause. I had been so afraid to confront her eyes, her likeness, that I neglected the most obvious of clues to the plot of her novel. It appeared to be for the relief of human trafficking in third world countries. Avila was starting to thank her friend, the woman who had been speaking earlier, for her dedicated work with the charity.

I felt like the most absolute jerk. My anxieties could have been cut off before they even sprouted if I hadn't been so proud and insistent on my victimhood.

I made my way to the exit and abruptly heard the sound of Avila's voice cut off as the door closed behind me.

As I made the short walk home, I contemplated the events of that week, that past decade. Could it be that simple? Could every song, and book, and show have misled me? Surely, if any ex would be vindictive and punitive, Avila should have been. Could it have been as easy to explain as an inflated memory, a trumped-up feeling that I was living within and experiencing every nuance of, instead of facing reality? Could a woman really just move on and wish a man well after a romantic dissolution? Where was the nervous laughter and the panicked breath? No music abruptly ended or picked up as I had approached. Could it be that she gave me no thought? Not enough to dedicate a year of writing to exact a bitter and protracted revenge.

Perhaps it was all just another game that I can't win, I thought. *Heartbreak, a meaningful career, a dead-end ambition. I can't win.* I think it was at that moment that I was released.

What will I do with myself now that I am robbed of my all-encompassing distraction? The wind extinguished from my sails as I was freed from the parasitic relationship I'd constructed with my vision of Avila. Could we both be free, rid of each other, and able to move on? How true-to-life, and how anticlimactic that seemed to me. But oh, what a relief to be just someone in her past and no longer in her path.

So why am I continuing? Why are you still reading? What more could there be to say? Come on, surely it must be plain-as-day to you. You must have an itch in the back of your mind insisting that something is still off, not quite right, "doesn't add up."

You're right.

I spent that Saturday and Sunday in a deep sleep, recuperating from my week of anxiety-induced insomnia. I felt refreshed and clean. I had faced my demon and she was nothing but an apparition held in between two opposing gusts of wind, suspended between their forces, but now, swept away.

As the morning sun sparkled off of the glittering skyline, I had an unyielding sense of unease. It was a bad omen to start the work week.

Perhaps my immune system had been thrown off by the emotional roller coaster of the previous week, I thought. However, this worry was not a phantom, reverberating and demanding to be remembered. The long email in my inbox revealed that I was indeed being taunted and that my worries were founded. I had spent all of my energy on Avila that I made no room in my mind to realize the obvious. The suspect I had been chasing was baiting me all along.

It was a note from the Traveler. With his text he applauded my efforts through veiled metaphors and back-handed asides. He had desired a worthy adversary to catch him. When he went to make another fraudulent transaction the previous week and discovered that his usual sites had been shut down, he left town immediately. He hinted at his arduous journey abroad and dared me to break all jurisdictional precedent and track him down.

I showed the message to Director Knight. He laughed at the hubris of this man and suggested that I go on and call up my counterpart at Interpol to begin tracking him. "Hobbertson, you're a competitive fellow. You run all those miles each week, and for what? Now you have someone to run after. Go get 'em."

What followed was a whirlwind of international exchanges and at least two last-minute trips to apprehend this man, only to find that he had just fled. With the ever-changing nature of money laundering and the now receding boundaries of the world, I find that I am spending more time at work and traveling than at home. It is time to dismantle the life I've built in this city of mine and make the leap. I'm moving to Washington, D.C, and I'll rent a crummy tiny apartment that I will never see. I'll finally be able to move up in my career and take the actions I need to, so that I can catch this taunting hacker.

I've spent the past few months unburying from the enormous wall I'd erected around myself. I have now read each of the Scarlett Moore novels and can say that they are indeed good. I've even watched the latest movie in the series. I don't see a trace of myself in them, but they have allowed me to re-learn who Avila was and appreciate our time together. I've learned to stop holding the opinions of other so highly and to forgive myself. I've learned to stop holding my breath for the next layer in a prolonged drama. It has ended.

When I look back now, I can see that week had been the fever-pitch. It had been one prolonged fitful sleepless night when the infection was at its worst; when the fever induced by Avila's memory was about to break. I recall that I had been in a cold sweat that entire week, my heart beating irregularly, and my joints tense. But now, it is over. It is a memory.

Releasing myself from the worry of Avila chasing me allowed me to realize that the man I was after, Traveler, was trying to ploy me into a cat-and-mouse game. He didn't just want to take off with the money, he wanted to have someone chase him. He needed the thrill of escape. Once I was released from the grip that I imagined, I was able to focus all of my energies on catching this man. Now he would have to worry about my motives and my next move. He would have to escape Trevor Hobbertson.

Author's Note

Back in 2016 I had a goal to release another book out one year after my debut novel, *Nailbiters*, was published. I had several short stories already written but I wanted to add one more to the collection. Escaping Avila Chase was inspired by several things, but one idea that really kicked it off was my husband getting questions from people after reading *Nailbiters*, "Are you afraid? She wrote a scary book!"

Escaping Avila Chase took on a life of its own and it also provided me with a new challenge. Writing a story from a male point of view. I very carefully and meticulously worked on this story. I had it in my mind that it was a long short story, but in reality, it is a novella.

I had *The Games You Cannot Win* complete and ready to go. I was going to be tight, but a week before my deadline, October 19, 2016, I set the pre-order for my book to launch exactly one year after *Nailbiters*. This collection was scheduled to release on October 26, 2016, exactly one year after my debut. It was a super short pre-order window, but my audience was super small at the time. It was more important for me to reach my goal than to follow best practices. I knew it was the final week that I would push for pre-orders anyways. I had a schedule in mind for continuing to post about the book until launch day.

But the day after I submitted the book, I got a call from my mom in the middle of the workday. My dad was diagnosed with lung cancer back in 2011. He beat it twice. But it came back a third time. He was still feeling okay, but the doctors weren't sure what to do next. I knew this might be it. I booked a plane ticket to go see him in early November, after my launch. But this call was a few weeks too early. He was in bad shape and I could hear it in my mom's voice. This was it.

My husband left work early, we packed up the car, and drove seven hours to get to my parent's house. My dad was in the hospital, and while still alive, not conscious. The next day he came home for hospice and by October 23rd, he was gone.

Of all the things I was thinking about in the days that followed, my book was the farthest from my mind. Even after we drove home, even after I flew up to visit my mom and help her start to clean the house up, my launch day came and went and I didn't post a thing. How could I pretend everything was okay when the worst thing had just happened? How could I ask people to buy my book, when all I wanted was to buy more time with my dad?

I wasn't focused on the launch or marketing the book afterwards. And if anything, thinking about *The Games You Cannot Win* will always make me think of losing my dad. It's the book I promote the least, and that's why.

Which means this story that I was so proud of, the story that most reviewers agree is the best in the series, doesn't get any attention. It doesn't reach people the way I intended.

So, I'm giving it a second chance. On the 5 year book birthday for *The Games You Cannot Win*, I am releasing *Escaping Avila Chase* as a standalone novella. I hope you enjoyed the story and will consider leaving a review or recommending it to a friend.

Thank you
M.K. Williams

Acknowledgments

I first want to give a big thank you to everyone who took a chance on reading a collection of short stories by an unknown indie author back in 2016. Your reviews and feedback helped me as an author and inspired me to release *Escaping Avila Chase* to stand on her own.

Next, I want to thank those who have been supporting my work. The cliché of the penniless writer persists for a reason, royalties are slim for even the best of us. Those who have taken the time and continued to financially support me through my Buy Me A Coffee membership have helped to keep me going. Thank you so much to Jason, Teresa, and Sheila for your support!

ABOUT THE AUTHOR

M.K. Williams is the author of multiple novels, self-publishing guides, and short stories. You can follow her for more in-depth information on these books at 1mkwilliams.com. To receive updates on upcoming books, please take a moment to subscribe.

If you enjoyed this story, please consider leaving a review for *Escaping Avila Chase*. Each review helps other readers discover this book. Thank you for your support.

www.ingramcontent.com/pod-product-compliance
Lightning Source LLC
Chambersburg PA
CBHW021740190726
48288CB00009B/3118